UNDER THE GYPSY MOON

Also by Lawrence Thornton

Imagining Argentina
Unbodied Hope: Narcissism and the Modern Novel

UNDER THE GYPSY MOON

Lawrence Thornton

DOUBLEDAY

New York   London   Toronto   Sydney   Auckland

PUBLISHED BY DOUBLEDAY

a division of Bantam Doubleday Dell Publishing Group, Inc.
666 Fifth Avenue, New York, New York 10103

DOUBLEDAY and the portrayal of an anchor with a dolphin
are trademarks of Doubleday,
a division of Bantam Doubleday Dell Publishing Group, Inc.

This novel is a work of fiction. Any references to historical events; to
real people, living or dead; or to real locales are intended only to give
the fiction a sense of reality and authenticity. Other names,
characters, places, and incidents either are the product of the author's
imagination or are used fictitiously, and their resemblance, if any, to
real-life counterparts is entirely coincidental.

DESIGNED BY ANNE LING

Library of Congress Cataloging-in-Publication Data

Thornton, Lawrence, 1937–
    Under the gypsy moon / by Lawrence Thornton. — 1st ed.
    p.   cm.
    I. Title.
PS3570.H6678U54   1990
813'.54—dc20   90-32470
                                                             CIP

ISBN 0-385-24706-0

Printed in the United States of America

October 1990

FIRST EDITION

BG

For Ed Loomis

Acknowledgments

I am grateful to the John Simon Guggenheim Foundation and the National Endowment for the Arts for fellowships that allowed me to complete this book.

For material on the Spanish Civil War and the German occupation of Paris I acknowledge the help of Ian Gibson, *The Death of Lorca*; Herbert Rutledge, *Guernica! Guernica!*; Blake Ehrlich, *Resistance*; and James Wilkinson, *The Intellectual Resistance in Europe*.

Special thanks are due to my wife, Toni Clark; my agent, Ned Leavitt; and my editor, David Gernert, for their many fine insights and warm encouragement.

Green, I want you green.
Green wind. Green boughs.
The ship on the sea
and the horse in the mountains.
· · · · · · · · · · ·
Under the gypsy moon
the things are looking at her
and she cannot look at them.
· · · · · · · · · · ·
Green, I want you green.
Big rimefrost stars
come with the shadow fish
that opens the path of dawn.
The fig tree rubs its belly
with the rasp of its branches
and the mountain, a thieving cat,
bristles its angry spikes.
· · · · · · · · · · ·
—Three hundred dark roses
spread over your white shirt.
Your blood smells and oozes
around your sash.
But I am no more my self
and my house is no more my house.
· · · · · · · · · · ·
An icicle of moonlight
supports her on the water.
Drunken Civil Guards
were beating on the door.
Green, I want you green.
Green wind. Green boughs.
The ship on the sea.
The horse in the mountains.

—from "Romance Sonámbulo"
Federico García Lorca

PART 1

LISBON
Hotel Ferdinand
November 23, 1942

1

Who knows where memory begins? Who can say where the vibrant voice becomes an echo, the face once so vividly intaglioed on the retina a fading copy in the mind?

Three weeks ago I had neither the desire nor the need to know.

Three weeks ago, when we left the Gare d'Austerlitz, and Paris slowly disappeared behind the snow, I had abandoned memory. I believed only in the future as Claude and Monika, Joaquín and I headed south to Lisbon, where a ship would take us away from the war to America. The jeopardy we'd endured was already blanketed by falling snow, silenced by whiteness that offered itself like a bright new page of life.

I have spent every day since our arrival watching ships leaving Lisbon's harbor, trying to distract myself by attending to their shapes and sluggish movements, but it does no good. Everything I see is filmed by memory, which rises like Lazarus to mock me for my presumption. Though I accept this censure, I insist that I did not part lightly with the past. For many years my life was devoted to its twists and turns. I knew its hidden chambers with the certain knowledge of a connoisseur, and walked away only when it was safe to think that the four of us would soon stand together at the ship's railing and watch Lisbon fall behind. It was neither short-sighted nor naive to believe I'd escaped. Everything had been planned, every contingency imagined. Without the benefit of the fortune-teller's art, how could we have known that a horse and rider waited in the mountains we had to pass through on our way to freedom?

It would be easy to blame chance for Joaquín's death, rather than the Guardia Civil. Easy to spend my days rocking back and forth in silence, an anguished woman clutching a photograph in my hands. Easy to wear grief like a black mantilla thrown across my shoulders.

But grief makes chance victorious, allows his great blank face to obscure Joaquín as surely as the moon's shadow sometimes falls upon the sun. I refuse that eclipse, and that is why I have taken up this diary.

Until this morning, when I knew I had to write, I dreaded the crossing to America as a final sundering, a last, watery farewell.

No more. Now I see it as a time to purge grief's bitterness with the pith and essence of Joaquín's life.

So I return to memory, not as the slave I was, but as its mistress. The white page that so recently offered itself to me will hold a different, sadder story than the one I was ready to inscribe. But it will have its benefactions, and of these none will be greater than the picture of a man neither Nazis nor Guardia Civil could silence. Perhaps, in a humble way, my words may act as epilogue to Joaquín's famous *Letters to Lorca*. Perhaps, by facing memory unafraid, I may find the way to look forward once again.

2

I have it on the harbor master's authority that our ship will leave by the end of the week. Time enough to build a foundation to sustain me on the crossing. Time enough to explain why Joaquín went to Granada and sought out the place where Lorca died, and in doing so altered the direction of his life and mine as well.

His journey to the place the Spaniards call Fuente Grande began one spring morning in Paris in 1936, a little over six years ago. By then his reputation as a novelist had spread across Europe and brought a letter inviting him to read and comment on his work at a writer's congress that summer in Madrid. The congress was a prestigious affair reserved for the best of the avant-garde, and the invitation, written by the president, a man named Carnero, was filled with pleasant flatteries.

o

It arrived on the heels of the publication of *Morning*, the second novel of a projected quartet devoted to the life of Paris. It should have been a happy time. The reviews were splendid, his publisher had fêted him, but depression set in even before the book's release. At the time he thought it was because he'd reached an impasse. He had written a thousand pages tracing the city's psyche through his narrator's dispassionate Germanic precision. He had given Heinz a painter's eye, a musician's ear to record all he saw and heard, but he feared these were not enough to sustain the next two books, which had to rise above the others and comprehend the whole.

His old friend, Jacques St. Omer, the essayist, laughed when Joaquín confided his troubles to him.

"Postpartum blues, Wolf. Everyone feels the same when they've just finished something. Don't be stupid. Get out of Paris for a while. Enjoy yourself. When you come back everything will look different."

There was no one Joaquín respected more. He and St. Omer had met soon after he arrived in Paris and quickly established a deep friendship, seeing each other at least once a month at Jacques's house where his wife stuffed them with food and the children took shameful advantage of his good nature. St. Omer was a French Algerian who emigrated to Europe when he was eighteen, working out his passage in the engine room of a filthy steamer. In Paris he survived by his wits, read voraciously, and finally became a respected journalist. It was St. Omer whom Joaquín turned to for advice when he began the quartet. They argued over his theories, shouted, insulted each other, but when *Dawn* was finished St. Omer took it to a well-known publisher and insisted that he read the first chapter as Jacques paced back and forth like an expectant father. Although the book needed no one's intercession, Joaquín was grateful. Every year, on the anniversary of its publication, he sent St. Omer a bottle of fine champagne.

He knew that he should take his old friend's advice, but

Joaquín was dedicated to his work. Abandoning Paris, even for a few weeks, went against the grain until he realized that he could accomplish nothing in his present state of mind. Then he wrote to Carnero, accepting the offer, and sent a longer letter to his aunt María in Madrid, asking if he could spend a few weeks with her and his uncle Pedro. She responded immediately, saying he was welcome to stay as long as he wished.

Rather than going directly to Madrid he decided to spend a few days visiting his father in Berlin, whom he hadn't seen since his mother's funeral several years earlier. He had never been close to Heinrich. After Joaquín turned his back on the family's bank, leaving Germany with the idea of becoming a writer, Heinrich refused to correspond with him for years, giving in only after Estrella fell ill and begged him to heal the rift. When Joaquín returned after her death he was shocked by the depth of his father's grief. The old man had always been indifferent to Estrella, treating her with only slightly less disdain than he did the servants, but he seemed to have forgotten this as soon as Joaquín arrived. Heinrich depended on him for everything, begged him to make the funeral arrangements. That night he insisted on sitting up late as he recalled the high points of his married life and drank himself unconscious. The next morning the old man greeted Joaquín in the breakfast room with an icy stare, and he knew their rapprochement had ended.

"He has a place for everything in his life," Joaquín told me once. "His mind is like an old-fashioned desk studded with drawers where his emotions are neatly stored—excitement, anger, desire, grief and the rest neatly labeled in Gothic script. Father is nothing if not systematic. After Mother died, he opened the grief drawer and emptied it of memories, tears, self-pity—everything he felt, or thought he should feel. I don't know if he experienced any of those emotions, or simply put them on for the occasion. In any case, the morning after the funeral he looked in, found the drawers empty, and resumed his life as Heinrich Wolf, banker and financier."

The city Joaquín abandoned, the city he remembered as it appeared six years earlier from a car in his mother's funeral cortège and then the high windows of his family's estate as he listened to Heinrich's brooding recollections, had undergone a profoundly disturbing change. At that time he was still essentially innocent of politics, though a few years earlier he had been outraged by reports of the torchlight parade of students to the square on Unter den Linden opposite the university where thousands of books had been burned. He knew that Hitler was meticulously obliterating the past in other, equally repugnant ways, but he was not prepared for the transformation of the city into a Fascist nightmare when he arrived that hot and sultry afternoon.

He had decided to stay in a hotel so there would be a retreat in the event things went badly with his father. That spring Berlin had begun cleaning itself in preparation for the Olympic games, but only the city's gardens and spacious avenues had been refurbished and neutralized. On the way in from the station he saw a few racist signs whose sickening impact did not strike with full force until after he unpacked and went out. He walked for block after block, passing grocery stores and butcher shops, bakeries and cafés, all shouting in German and Hebrew: JEWS NOT ADMITTED. JEWS ENTER THIS PLACE AT THEIR OWN RISK.

At a favorite coffee house he opened a newspaper to read while he ate a roll. The language of the signs seemed modest compared with the xenophobia of the official press. He put the paper down in disgust, listened to conversations that seemed drawn from what he'd read, picked the paper up again, unable to believe the hatred.

On the way back to his hotel a Jewish woman and her two children approached from the opposite direction. They seemed to have no destination and walked as if in a daze. He was ashamed when their eyes met, wished he'd never gone out.

"She stared, but not like beggars when someone well-off comes by," Joaquín told me. "She had no hope of gain. That was the terrible thing. She stared, and I knew that was all she could do. She had been ordered into silence. Her hands were frightened so that they couldn't even reach for a coin if it were offered. I looked at her hands and then I watched her go up the street. In a little while I ran after her, overcome with guilt. She turned and pulled her children close, as if I was about to harm them. She said nothing, not a word. It was all in her eyes. I gave her the bills I had in my wallet, stuffing them into her bag when she wouldn't take them. Then I turned away. Do you understand? I left because I couldn't look at her anymore. I still see her wordless mouth."

As soon as he reached his father's house it was clear that the old man was not happy to see him. His hair had gone as white as an eggshell in the last six years, and there were bushy white clouds for eyebrows. Joaquín hoped he might have mellowed now that he was an octogenarian, but he still bore a grudge against his son for having turned his back on the family business.

"It would have been better if you'd stayed here," he said at dinner. "If not for me, then for your mother. Instead you surround yourself with hedonists and pederasts. I saw Paris once, and could not leave soon enough."

Joaquín let him go on, knowing that his resentment would blow itself out. Besides, he was more interested in what Heinrich had to say about the present situation than the old rift between them. Later that evening he asked his father's opinion about the Nazi decrees. Heinrich looked at him blankly. He said that the bank was thriving and he was happy.

"You condone the racial laws?"

Heinrich looked over the top of his wineglass.

"There are excesses," he answered as he put down the glass and lighted a cigar. "But necessity outweighs them. You have never been much in the world, Joaquín, like your mother. On the other hand, the world is my life. If you understood finance you would know about Jews. Things are better now, and they will improve."

For as long as he could remember, his father's distaste for what he called Levantines had been obvious. He even refused to see some of Estrella's family, distant cousins from the country, because of their Moorish features. An argument would have served no purpose, but Joaquín felt tainted. As Heinrich went on he remembered the woman and her children, and that was when he knew he could stay no longer. As soon as he could, he said that he was tired. Heinrich did not seem to mind when he left. He took the long way around to his hotel, thinking about his father. As a child, Heinrich's attitudes had seemed odd and ungenerous. Now they disgusted him. Long before he reached the hotel he decided to cut the visit short.

He was studying the train schedule the next morning when the phone rang. It was his cousin, Albert, inviting him to dinner, and he gladly accepted. That day he spent wandering through the city, confirming impressions that left him full of indignation when he arrived at Albert's house. His cousin worked as an engineer for Krupp and had never left Berlin. He made a few poor jokes about Joaquín as prodigal son, but he was interested in hearing about the life of Paris, and Joaquín obliged. Albert and his wife were staunch burghers whose circumscribed life seemed comically claustrophobic, but it was better being with them than with his father. Dinner passed pleasantly enough, and afterward Albert suggested coffee and cognac in the living room. As he poured their drinks he asked Joaquín how long he was staying. When he replied that he was leaving the next day Albert said, "It's a pity you can't stay for the games. We expect great victories, you know."

Sports bored Joaquín, but Albert had distinguished himself in school as a sprinter.

"I only wish I were fifteen years younger," Albert added nostalgically. "It would be a pleasure to run against negroes."

Then he began expounding the virtues of the Reich, his eyes flashing as ideas surfaced in a complex righteousness. Joaquín told me that he felt as if vengeance, or something worse, had entered the room. He listened as long as he could. Then, frustrated and angry, he told Albert about his encounter with the woman.

"The sooner they leave or die the better, as far as I'm concerned."

He and Albert were clearly on a collision course, but he could not be quiet after what had happened with his father, and so he asked Albert what he thought of Hitler.

"A great man. A monument!"

"He's nothing but a psychotic martinet."

Amazement spread across Albert's face as he slammed down his glass.

"Get out! I won't hear treason in my home."

As Joaquín stood, Albert rose from his chair and they remained there for a moment, simply looking at each other. Joaquín said that Albert's eyes were very bright. That he was smug.

"There's no place for misfits here. Your father's right. Yes, we talk about you from time to time. It shouldn't come as a surprise. You've disgraced him, but you were always out of step, even when we were children."

"I'll leave now," Joaquín said. He wanted to reach the door as fast as possible.

"Not before I tell you what I think."

"Yes?"

"A German would understand, but you have mixed blood. I wonder if you're even half German, or if that was only put forward to save the family honor."

"Meaning?"

"Only that perhaps your mother slept with another Spaniard, or even a Jew. There would have been time with your father gone so much."

Joaquín stepped forward and struck Albert in the face. The blow sent him careening backward into the chair, which toppled over. His nose was broken and blood gushed down his face, staining his shirt and sweater. Joaquín was standing over him, waiting for him to get up, when the door opened. Hilda screamed as she ran to her husband, who whimpered as he touched his broken nose. She shouted at Joaquín as he turned and went to the door. He had never struck anyone in his adult life. He was appalled, but he was also strangely jubilant as he closed the door with an aching hand and hurried down the stairs.

The night was filled with lurid dreams which he remembered vividly, recounting them to me much later as if they'd plagued him only the night before. His father stood on his desk and ordered him to climb into a drawer. He heard the key in the lock, his father's laughter, Albert's. Heinz spoke from the pages of *Dawn* and *Morning.* He knew that he had not written the words. Albert tilted his brandy snifter so that Joaquín could see the amber liquid. The Jewish woman's face floated up from the bottom as Albert lit a match and, with a headwaiter's flourish, set her face on fire. He laughed. Always Heinz was present, reading lines he'd never written.

He woke exhausted and trembling and lay there for a long time. Of all the dreams, those with Heinz troubled him most deeply. He dismissed the crude symbolism of the others. They gave him nothing he did not already know. But Heinz mocked him with unintelligible words whose meaning he nevertheless inferred. He had lived like a sleepwalker on the surface of things. It seemed to Joaquín that his work was consuming itself out of guilt and innocence. His understanding took him no further for several weeks, but he had reached a threshold. Berlin was a door which had swung open unexpectedly, its hinges creaking with his father's laughter, Albert's, the tramp of booted feet. It swung open in the silence of the woman's mouth, opened into Spain and Paris where Lorca and I waited, holding his destiny in our hands.

●

Two days later, on Monday, Joaquín arrived at the main railway station in Madrid. Even as he stepped down from his car he knew that the relief he'd hoped to find had been an illusion. No vicious signs were posted there, but the somber mood of the people moving quietly under the eyes of the Guardia Civil was unmistakable. The rumors of civil war that had reached Paris and which he had dismissed in the belief that cooler heads would finally prevail came to life now in the almost preternatural quiet, the arrogant and threatening presence of the Guardia, the averted eyes and suspicious stares of peasants and working people and a few aristocrats. He was prepared for none of it. How could it have been otherwise? In the space of four days he had seen too much, said too much, dreamed too much. Until he went to Berlin he had thought that his dual heritage fitted seamlessly into his life, that the intentions of his work, the long days of exploration and writing, expressed what was best in him. As he made his way to the exit he knew he was in the grip of something more powerful, as if what he'd seen and heard in Berlin was mixed with the life of the crowd. When he looked at the Guardia he saw jackbooted Nazis. When he stepped aside for a couple with a baby he saw the Jewish woman. He was fascinated. He was appalled. He understood, and he was ignorant. The solid footing of his life had shifted in the bizarre dream of Heinz's accusations and the dark moods he sensed in Madrid. He felt like a swimmer coming up for air when he reached the taxi stand and gave the driver directions to María's house. As they pulled away from the curb the strangeness that had seized him inside the station receded. He breathed more freely. He had received an education in Berlin that was being continued now in Spain. That was good. He wanted to see clearly. He had encountered his own creative spirit in Heinz's mysterious accusations. That too was good. He wanted to understand himself. The only mistake he made as he traveled through the city into the suburbs toward the retreat of his aunt's house was in thinking that he was still in control of his destiny.

Since the congress would not convene until Thursday there
was ample time to settle into the old house on a tree-lined street
far from the commotion of the city. The downstairs rooms gave
onto a shaded patio he had loved since childhood, and it was
there he spent the first afternoon with his aunt and uncle.

María had put on weight since he last saw her. Her hair was
streaked with white, and she wore it pulled back in a bun so that
it fitted her head like a cap, emphasizing the structure of her
face and her piercing eyes, which were sad now because of her
husband's illness. A stroke had left Pedro in a dozing silence
broken only occasionally by disjointed comments. His sense of
time was eroded, and she no longer attempted to correct his
chronologies. It was lonely, she said, and Joaquín's arrival was a
blessing. As she filled their glasses with sangria he studied his
uncle's serene face as he slept in a chair by the fountain.

"I'm very sorry."

"It was God's will. At least he is in no pain, and sometimes
he is quite lucid for a few minutes. Then it is more painful when
he slips away. I tell myself that I should be grateful he lived such
a full life, but it does not always do much good. I have learned
not to dwell on it. Now. Tell me about your father. Is he well?"

"Money keeps him going." He considered telling her about
Heinrich's appalling attitudes, but María knew his father and
would not have been surprised. He still felt abraded by their
encounter and decided to make a joke of it. "He'll stay alive as
long as he sees his interest compounding."

"Ah, yes, that is Heinrich. I saw that mania in him the first
time we met, that and his rigidity. You had the same tightness of
soul when you were a child, you know, when your family came
here in the summer. I saw a little burgher arrive. Then, after a
few days, you seemed relieved, more yourself. Do you remember
when Pedro gave you a suit of lights? There was a gleam in your
eyes when you came out with it on. I thought to myself, He
wants a little adventure, a taste for the arena."

She glanced at him, hesitating before going on.

"Is there any torero left, or are you all Heinz now?"

It was the kind of question only an aunt could ask. He remembered those visits very clearly. Though it was always hot in Madrid, his father insisted on wearing a blazing white shirt and a proper tie. His monocle sometimes slipped out of place and fell the length of its black ribbon. His mother wore handkerchiefs soaked with eau de cologne which she used to daub at her neck and the cleavage between her breasts. Sometimes she called him to her and wiped his face with the soft linen. He could still recall the scent.

"All boys are toreros for a while. But we grow up, you know. Look at these gray hairs."

"It would not hurt to feel that part of yourself once in a while, Joaquín. I read your books, and for page after page I see nothing but your German blood. It is all very brilliant, of course, and I am proud and tell my friends about your latest triumph. For a long time I did not think about your suit of lights. Then, a few months ago, my friend Isabel said that your Heinz had a spiritual brother, a character in some Englishman's book whose philosophy is summed up in the phrase, 'Look on and make no sound.' It worries me a little. Even your father has commitments. I don't mean to insult you, only to say what is on my mind."

She had quite innocently led him back to Berlin, to the train station. He had lived with Heinz for six years as if in a second skin. To a certain degree he was Heinz, and now he felt again, with a renewed sense of strangeness, that he had compromised himself, or had been blinded by Heinz's easy eloquence, his lofty theories. He knew that María was not accusing him of disloyalty, but he could not say the same for himself.

"That's how the ideas come out," he answered lamely.

"May I say something else?"

"Of course."

"Can you afford to stand so far away? Times are changing. You know what the Guardia did to the workers in Casas Viejas?

It was a bloodbath. Things will be bad here, too, in France and Germany. You are not Pedro, sleeping through the end of your life. God forgive me for saying so, but he would be better off dead because he no longer lives in this world. You write like an angel, but what if this Paris of yours changes? What then?"

•

On Thursday a taxi came for him at noon. An hour should have been more than enough time to reach the theater, but when they entered the city they were stopped by workers demonstrating in a square. When Joaquín asked the driver to take a detour, the man threw up his hands. "Look over there."

More people had poured into the intersection, blocking the nearby streets. "I don't blame them," the driver said. "It's impossible to live anymore."

The driver was cursing Franco when a detachment of Guardia Civil appeared and in a matter of minutes broke up the crowd. Three soldiers grabbed a man running in front of the taxi and began beating him with clubs until blood welled like a carnation from his face. Without thinking Joaquín got out. One of the soldiers motioned for him to come closer as the man on the ground raised his hand to shield his head from another blow. "Leave him alone!" Joaquín shouted. In response the soldier struck him a glancing blow on the forehead. He staggered back to the taxi. As he pressed a handkerchief against the wound he saw his assailant's club rise and come down.

Fortunately the crowd had dispersed enough for the driver to get through. On the far side of the square he glanced at Joaquín in the rearview mirror.

"That was very brave, señor. Are you all right?"

"Yes. Fine. Just a tiny cut."

At the theater Joaquín hurriedly got out and tipped the driver extra for his wasted time.

"Bless you, señor. If you come again, and I find you, I will give you a free ride, anywhere you want to go. But watch out now. Things are going to happen."

Joaquín stepped up onto the sidewalk. "Thanks for getting me here. And fuck the Guardia."

The driver beamed. "Yes, that's it! Fuck the Guardia!"

It was cool inside. Until his eyes adjusted to the dim light the walls were scarcely more than black planes receding downward to the yellow square of the stage. A musty scent combined with smoke and the odors of sweat and perfume. He touched his wound gingerly. There was a slight swelling, and it was tender. He remembered María's comments about Casas Viejas as he edged through the crowd and made his way to the stage where a plump man with a pencil mustache rushed over and identified himself as Constantino Ruiz Carnero.

"I recognized you from your photograph," he said. Then he noticed the cut. "My God, what happened?"

"A demonstration. One of the Guardia took exception to my looks."

Carnero shook his head sadly.

"It happens all the time now," he said. "Some people think it will blow over, but I say we're headed for war."

"Yes, probably." Joaquín had a sudden intense desire to return to the peace and quiet of Paris.

"Well, come on then, it's time to start. Everyone is waiting to hear you."

A poet and an essayist went first. The poet read his work slowly, with great feeling. The essayist presented a manifesto for cleaning the slate of old methods. His voice was deep and melodious, and Joaquín worried about matching its dignity. He rarely spoke Spanish except in a café he frequented on weekends. While the essayist continued, Joaquín bent over his own translation of *Dawn*, carefully pronouncing each word of the description of first light on the Passage des Panoramas where Heinz sees all the faces of Paris superimposed on the glass dome.

He was a great success. Afterward most of the questions were directed to him and he answered as well as he could, but he was glad when Carnero finally stood up and closed the meeting. His head still hurt and he was looking forward to a quiet evening. María had promised paella for dinner, and her special flan.

People had gathered at the stage with copies of his books, and after he finished autographing he gathered his papers together and turned to leave when he saw a man sitting in the front row who was obviously waiting for him. He was quite thin, and his rumpled linen suit looked a little too large for his frail body. More than anything else about him, Joaquín was struck by the way the man's hair receded from a widow's peak which emphasized his dark eyes. As Joaquín descended the steps the man approached, complimented him on his work, and introduced himself as Federico Lorca as he reached into his pocket and took out a small volume, saying that he'd consider it an honor if Joaquín would accept it.

Lorca had given him a copy of the *Romancero Gitano*. Joaquín stammered that he had been reading Lorca's work ever since it became available in France. Lorca waved his hand in a self-deprecating way, and asked if he had time for a drink. When Joaquín said yes, Lorca took him by the arm, saying he knew a good bar just down the street.

They found a table on the sidewalk and spent the next two hours together. Joaquín told me there was a feeling of awkwardness at first and of surprise as well. Lorca seemed altogether too refined to have created such poems and plays.

"I have to admit that I expected a gypsy," Joaquín told him.

Lorca laughed and replied, "And I a dour German. You're much too affable."

They opened up to each other after that, admitting that what attracted them to the other's work was just its difference. The café was becoming crowded, but the newcomers did not bother them until four members of the Guardia Civil came swaggering up the sidewalk and took a table near the entrance. It had been noisy. Now everyone spoke in whispers. The

Guardia slouched in their chairs, enjoying the effect of their presence as they looked around, daring anyone to match their stares. Their uniforms were nut brown. Insignias in red and blue were sewn on collars and sleeves. Their jackets were cross-strapped with belts worn over the left shoulder, and the belts at their waists were closed with large gold buckles bearing insignia. It was their patent-leather hats that truly set them apart. In the distance they looked like tricorns, but they were really a sort of round skullcap with a visor at the back, turned up, like the hats banderillos wear. Joaquín thought that the uniforms, especially the hats, transformed otherwise unremarkable men, encouraging rudeness. Lorca was listening carefully to him, watching him. He wanted to know if one of them had attacked Joaquín earlier.

"I don't think so. But it's hard to say since they look alike. I only wish you didn't have to deal with them."

"We," Lorca corrected him. "We. All Spaniards now have to deal with them. There is no choice."

By that time many of the patrons had left. Those who remained looked uncomfortable. Lorca suggested that it might be best to go and Joaquín agreed.

It had grown dark and streetlamps made bright moons against the dirty fronts of buildings. As they walked to the taxi stand Joaquín admitted that Spain had changed for him. Not because of his wound, but because of the dark mood he sensed. The city he knew as a child now seemed like a place El Greco might have painted.

"That's one way to put it," Lorca said. "But for me it's like watching rain in the country, out in the vega beyond Granada. It makes no difference if you're on foot, riding a bicycle, driving. You see it coming, imagine those first drops before you feel them. But perhaps I'm getting carried away. Gypsy poets live too much in presentiments. If the rain gets too close, I'll make it a prisoner of words."

They had reached the taxi stand and Lorca told him he

would leave then. They shook hands and Joaquín said, "Be careful, Lorca. Those clubs are hard."

"I know. I'm off to Granada tomorrow. My friends say it's dangerous there, but if the Falangists make trouble I'll tell them that my friend Joaquín Wolf took the blow intended for me. That my account is paid in full."

"Come to Paris."

"I will. Maybe someday soon."

As Joaquín got into the taxi Lorca stood a moment on the curb. When he turned back in the direction of the café Joaquín saw the Guardia coming up the street. Lorca hesitated, as if he was unsure he should continue, but he went on.

The Guardia were drunk. One saw Lorca and said something to the others. Joaquín heard them laugh just as the driver started the motor.

"Stay a minute, please," he said.

Lorca passed the Guardia, and as he did one turned and shouted, "Hey, sweetheart!"

Lorca continued as if he had not heard the insult.

"Come on, sweetheart!" As the soldier shouted he reached down and grabbed his crotch. "I've got something you'll like!"

Lorca went on to the corner and then turned. Joaquín could see his face in the lamplight, and he told me Lorca seemed irritated, but not afraid. It occurred to him that he had heard it all before. He looked as if he were going to say something, then thought better of it.

"It's all right," Joaquín told the driver. "You can go."

As the taxi pulled away from the curb Lorca waved and vanished around the corner.

Joaquín's wound lay halfway between his left eyebrow and his hairline. The club had pressed his flesh, forcing it open, rather than cutting it cleanly, as would have been the case with a knife, so the wound was ragged, not so much a line or a tear as a semicircle, and it did not heal well. Although he cleaned it carefully that night in his bathroom, and felt the sting of tincture of iodine as María applied the medicine with tenderness and care, it would leave a scar. A week later the scab came off, and the bright pink flesh already had its shape. When he saw it in the mirror he thought his eyes were going bad. He bent closer, saw his face grow large and distorted until the scar was in perfect focus. It had taken the form of a hat of the Guardia Civil, a little round circle at one end of which was a straight section, like their reversed visors. He laughed at his misfortune, telling himself that it was only appropriate the Guardia had left its signature.

●

He had reason to remember that idea several days later. By then he'd settled into a pleasant routine which left his mornings free for reading and writing. He was in the patio making notes on the demonstration with the notion that he might use them for a story. It was very quiet and the water splashing in the fountain aided his concentration; then he heard a door open. As soon as he saw María he knew something was wrong. She looked distraught, and he was convinced that Pedro had taken a turn for the worse. He got up and went to her.

"What is it?"

"I'm so sorry," she said, handing him the newspaper. "Lorca has been killed. Here. They say he was betrayed to the Falange."

The headline shouted in boldface: THE EXECUTION OF THE GREAT POET GARCÍA LORCA HAS BEEN CONFIRMED. It had occurred outside Granada, in a place he had never heard of called Fuente Grande. He read the story twice, then carefully folded the paper. María touched his arm.

"Would you like me to stay, or leave you alone?"

"I think I'll go up to my room," he answered, but as soon as he got there he realized his mistake. The room made him feel as if he were suffocating, and so he dropped the paper on his bed and left. On the way downstairs he remembered Lorca turning the corner beneath the streetlight. He could not believe he was dead. It was preposterous, as if someone had told him that men were walking on the moon.

He wandered in the mottled shade of the old trees. As he crossed the street a car narrowly missed him and the driver stuck his head out the window, shouting an obscenity. Joaquín did not respond because just then the refrain of a ballad was repeating itself like a chiming clock. "At five in the afternoon, at precisely five in the afternoon." He had a terrible thought. Was it possible that they had killed Lorca at the hour made famous in his homage to Mejías? Much later he learned that none of the Falange had such vivid imaginations. Many could not even read, and those who could knew only the official version of Lorca's work— that it was decadent, antichurch, and praised the Gypsies. And so they did not make the hour of his death coincide with that of his old friend. Instead they followed the procedures laid down by Valdés, their leader in Granada. They marched him out to the barranca of Víznar at dawn when he could see the sun rising from behind the peaks of the Sierra de Harana, and the houses of Víznar were pink with morning light.

Joaquín found himself in a neighborhood of small shops and cafés. It occurred to him that coffee might help clear his mind, and so he took a table at a café that was deserted except for a young couple sitting outside who had moved their chairs close together. They were involved in a serious conversation, and the glasses on their table remained untouched. The girl wore a black beret and a tight black sweater with a scarf thrown over her shoulders. Her companion had on a good suit. He was speaking earnestly to her. Joaquín decided that he would sit where he could watch them in the hope that their seriousness might distract him. He shifted his chair so that he was looking directly at the entrance, and he watched until the girl glanced at him and held his eyes long enough to let him know she did not appreciate being observed that way. Then he tried to concentrate on the waiter as he took down the old menu and put up a new one. He tried to ritualize drinking his coffee. He thought that if he did everything very precisely he might be able to control his anger, the sense of rage and helplessness that had come upon him, but nothing helped. The act of raising the cup to his lips, the dark flavor of the coffee only intensified his emotions. He remembered the Guardia in the café, remembered them on the street. He tried to avoid the image of Lorca waving, but his white suit shone like a moth beneath the streetlight. His hand was raised in a farewell gesture, but he also seemed to be beckoning, and it was then he knew that he must go to Granada and see where Lorca died.

●

It made no difference that when I learned these things Joaquín had been safely back in Paris for three years. They had the feel of prophecy because I have never believed that what happens to us is governed solely by chance. No, I side with the Greeks who insisted that fate runs like a golden thread in the weaving of our lives. I know some design led both of them to Fuente Grande. Afterward Lorca's friends wrung their hands in consternation, convinced he could have stayed in Madrid, or found refuge in Majorca. But he was drawn to Granada, the city of Gypsies and black-robed priests, of the Alhambra and the Falange. I believe too that as Joaquín sat there in that café, bent over coffee he could not drink, his fate was woven into Lorca's on that golden thread. I defy anyone to say that what happened as a consequence was not destined.

●

Joaquín arrived in Granada sick at heart and filled with anger. When the bellboy let him into his hotel room and he saw the city spread out below he thought the view might calm him. He forced himself to study the iron scrollwork of balconies, the Alhambra rising like a Moorish patriarch above the roofs, but those felicities only made Lorca's fate more incomprehensible. At that moment he had no idea that the vertiginous pull of the crowd he had felt in the train station in Madrid was still at work. All he knew was that he had come to Granada on the strength of an emotion he did not fully understand except that it could not be ignored. He came to pay homage, to protest, to grieve over a senseless death. I have wondered about that often, since to me it seems so clearly a prelude, rather than a coda. But that is the virtue of hindsight. I believe he did not foresee any of the consequences, that he was like a swimmer who confidently enters the sea and does not know until it is too late that he has been caught in an undertow which will pull him farther out than he has ever gone before.

He rose early the next morning and had breakfast in the hotel patio. Since learning of Lorca's death, he had pieced together a reasonably accurate account of what happened from a variety of papers, but he was ignorant of the countryside, and when he finished eating he went inside and asked the clerk if someone could take him to Fuente Grande. The man looked at him guardedly, responding that the manager, Gonzales, might help, and returned a minute later with a balding, mustachioed man, very grave in demeanor.

When Joaquín said that he wanted to visit Fuente Grande Gonzales stared at him suspiciously.

"It's a personal matter," Joaquín added. Gonzales flipped through the register and ran his finger down the page to the column listing Joaquín's nationality. As soon as he saw *German* he relaxed.

"You must take a taxi. I'll call one."

Twenty minutes later an ancient Fiat pulled up. A portly man wearing a beret and a worn jacket came around to Joaquín's side and opened the door to the back seat.

"No," Joaquín said, shaking his head. "If you don't mind, I'll ride in front."

As they pulled away from the curb the driver put on sunglasses.

"There is some problem with my eyes. The doctor says the sun is not good for them, so every day is like evening to me, but there are worse things. Gonzales said you want to see Fuente Grande. Why?"

"To pay my respects to a friend."

"Who?"

"García Lorca."

"You knew him?"

"A little. Enough."

"I knew some of his friends," he said softly, as if it cost him something to release the words. "Some banderillos and a flamenco singer. Mergal, one of the banderillos, I grew up with. My brother, Lorenzo, was the singer."

He lapsed into silence then, glancing at Joaquín from time to time. Suddenly, as if it were too much to keep in, he burst out vehemently, "The Falange are swine. Franco is a swine. I am not afraid to say it. You know what I do every morning? I go to church and pray for his death."

He let go of the steering wheel with one hand and pinched up the sleeve of his tattered jacket.

"See this? I have others. A brown and a green, good quality, but I wear black because of how I feel. My brother died only because he had a conscience."

He went on then, and bitterness ran through his words like a stream of bile.

Before the war Lorenzo's flamenco troupe played in the best music halls. They had full bellies, large audiences, but their fortunes changed overnight when Spain began gnawing at herself like a dog in the street with a broken back. Lorenzo hated the Falange and the Guardia Civil. Soon he was acting as a courier for the Republicans, but it was not enough and he began singing rebel songs whenever he thought his audiences were sympathetic. It had gotten him in trouble but he did not care. By the time they arrived in Granada he had decided to disband the troupe after their engagement and exchange their guitars and songs for guns and bullets.

In the meantime they were grateful for the few pesos they'd earn in a run-down café. The owner let them use a storage room reeking with cheese and garlic to warm up in. Hector and Angel, the guitarists, played a little for the dancers, Dolores and Paco. Lorenzo sang a few granadianas to limber up his voice, and then they went out front to a badly lighted room full of people.

They were good that night. Lorenzo had sensed it in the back room, and they got better as they went along. Dolores had just finished a difficult dance and he was congratulating her when the Guardia burst through the front door and pushed their way toward the stage, knocking people left and right. Lorenzo's car was in the alley behind the café and he shouted to the others to follow him outside. There was a shot and Hector's guitar went to pieces, but they managed to get off the stage unharmed. As they ran through the storage room Lorenzo knocked over some sherry casks behind them and slammed the door, and they were headed for the car when the door opened again. A shaft of light bright as a new moon cut into the darkness as the Guardia fired and Dolores spun around like a rag doll before falling dead at Lorenzo's feet. A second later Angel stumbled against him, clutching his guitar and coughing blood. As Lorenzo yanked at the car door he felt a hand on his shoulder and then there was a tremendous sound in his head as the alley filled with light.

When he came to the next day three men dragged him into Colonel Valdés's office in the civil government building where Valdés read the charges and asked Lorenzo if he had anything to say. He knew who Valdés was. Everyone did. He had already achieved a certain fame for the power of his eyes because, to satisfy some perversity known only to him, he always forced his victims to look at him as he pronounced their sentences.

Lorenzo's vision was blurred. His head felt on fire. He knew that words were useless at that point, and so he cleared his throat and spat into Valdés's face. The colonel looked at him for several seconds, unable to believe the insult. Then his eyes filled with rage and he came out cursing from behind his desk, beating Lorenzo until he lost consciousness.

The driver paused then, glancing at Joaquín to judge the effect of his story.

"I found out where he was a few days later. For reasons I will never understand, they let me see him for an hour. That's why I know all this. He was very calm and said that he wanted me to listen carefully because we both knew what lay in store for him. Only when he reached the point where he was taken before Valdés did he waver. He said that he had seen eyes like those only once before in his life. They were huge, saffron-colored eyes, like those of the papier-mâché effigies of Ferdinand and Isabella carried through the streets of Barcelona during the festival of Corpus Christi when we were children. He used to watch the procession in utter terror as it made its way through the square to the church, even though our mother explained that they were only giant dolls carried by men concealed beneath gaudy robes. It was not their size that frightened him but their large, unblinking eyes. Even the hooded penitentes who walked the streets during Holy Week armed with staffs and flails had less power over his imagination than those walking dolls.

"That was the last time I saw him, but I can guess the rest. A few nights later they drove him and some other prisoners out past Víznar to Fuente Grande where they locked them up in an old house called La Colonia. Lorca was there. It was common knowledge."

He fell silent then and seemed to concentrate very intensely on his driving. Joaquín had been deeply moved by the story and said that he was sorry, but the cabbie only grunted a response. He was obviously lost in thought, and that was when what happened to Lorca became real. Until then Joaquín had only names of places. Now, in the silence, Valdés took shape before him. He could see Lorca and Lorenzo and the others in La Colonia as the city rolled by in a blur of shapes and colors.

Only when they reached the open country, the vega, did the driver speak again.

"Is it safe to tell you my name?"

"Of course."

"It is Bustamante, Francisco Rodríguez Bustamante. What do they call you?"

"Joaquín Wolf."

"Spanish?"

"My mother's side."

"I understand. We will find where my brother and your friend were shot, Joaquín. When we do," he added as he reached under the seat and pulled out a bottle, "when we do, it would be an honor to me if we drank a toast."

They were driving along a narrow road through the brown countryside. A low mountain range lay off in the distance, its peaks apparently without growth, like a mountain in the desert. As they drew closer Joaquín saw that sparse vegetation had taken hold two thirds of the way up, but the peak itself was nothing more than rocks and pale earth.

"It is very beautiful, at least to me," Bustamante said, gesturing toward the mountain. "I have looked at the Sierra de Alfacar all my life. Beyond it is the Sierra de Harana. Lorenzo and Federico died out there, between the villages of Alfacar and Víznar. I have not had the heart to go there, but someone in Víznar will help us. Would you like a drink?"

With that he pulled the cork with his teeth, removed it with his free hand, and tilted the bottle. When he finished he wiped its mouth on his sleeve and handed it to Joaquín. It was a fine amontillado, very clean and dry, and Joaquín took a long drink as they crawled through Alfacar and proceeded up a grade through olive groves.

He knew they were on Archbishop's Road. Every story he'd come across mentioned it and he felt a little knot of fear. As if reading his mind, Bustamante said, "This is the way they came every night. Before the Falange made Víznar famous for the dawn paseo, the walk of death, it was known only for its bakers, who make excellent bread and sell it in Granada. They still do, but now there is a special loaf—el negro, they call it. In every batch they send there is one loaf of black bread as a memento for those who were killed. Look. Víznar."

A sleepy village appeared on the hillside. Its steep street was lined with white houses that hurt the eyes. As they entered, Joaquín saw that the front walls of every house were lined with terra cotta pots of orange capsicums and geraniums. Bustamante pointed to a large building on the hill above the houses.

"The Archbishop Moscoso's summer palace. The Falange bastards made it their headquarters. Every night cars came up the road from Alfacar to Víznar with the rebels tied up in the back seats. Sometimes they stopped to do business in the palace, maybe even to kill a few. No one knows for sure. There are those who say it is haunted now."

A minute later they stopped in front of a whitewashed cantina with two windows and a narrow, beaded doorway directly on the street.

"I will ask directions."

Joaquín got out and watched Bustamante disappear behind the curtain. He decided to stretch his legs and walked slowly to the end of the street. The village seemed to exist out of time. He was thinking about why that was so when he saw Bustamante motioning angrily at him.

"They are all cowards," he said when they were back in the car. "No one would offer himself as a guide. We will have to find it ourselves."

"What did they say?"

"Only that it is beyond the end of Archbishop's Road. They told me they had not been there, but I do not believe it."

"What are they afraid of? The Guardia? I haven't seen any since we left the city."

As Bustamante glanced at him Joaquín saw his reflection in the sunglasses, which were not large enough to disguise the man's impatience.

"Everyone is always afraid of the Guardia, señor. It is only prudent. But remember these are peasants, and peasants are superstitious."

"That is what you meant about the palace?"

"Yes. They are always more afraid of things they cannot see."

With that he put the car in gear and Víznar fell behind as they climbed the low hills overlooking the valley dotted with pines and olive groves. The bald peak of the Sierra de Alfacar rose straight ahead, imparting a disinterested serenity to the scene which somehow magnified the sense of foreboding Joaquín felt about Bustamante's remarks. He was not superstitious, and held no belief in the supernatural. Moreover, there had been nothing in the appearance of the archbishop's palace to encourage uneasiness. All things considered, it seemed rather unremarkable as the summer home of such an eminence. He had begun to attribute his emotion to the way Bustamante had spoken of it as haunted for the peasants, as if he halfway believed it himself, when the truth struck him. The barranca of Víznar was very close, though he could not see it yet. He realized that in his haste to reach Granada, to find transport to Fuente Grande, he had not prepared himself to see the place where Lorca died. That, undoubtedly, was why he felt vulnerable, and he wondered how he was going to manage his feelings when he finally came face to face with the barranca.

Bustamante stopped to consult his map. As he traced the red line of the road with his finger Joaquín studied the peak of the Sierra de Alfacar. A few lone pines and nondescript plants grew between boulders, making the nakedness more apparent. There was something sinister about the denuded mountain, and he was glad when Bustamante drove on. He rolled down his window and heard the plash of water from the *acequia* running alongside the road. Then they passed into a grove of trees sheltering an old stone and timber building roofed with tiles.

"La Colonia," Bustamante said. "It used to be a place for the children of the wealthy in the summer. We can walk now."

He retrieved his bottle, got out and spread the map on the hood where he studied it, pointed, and went ahead without another word.

They followed the watercourse and crossed a stone bridge where the water rushed across a small aqueduct.

"The barranca?" Joaquín asked.

"Just ahead, I think."

Now the road and the watercourse curved together around the hill into an open space where pale earth was dotted with young pines, hardly more than saplings. Joaquín could make out indentations in the ground.

"Their graves," Bustamante said. "I knew that if I ever came out here this is how I would recognize the spot."

They went into the olive grove shading the teardrop-shaped pool of Ainadamar. Everything Joaquín had read coalesced in his mind then, and he saw, with startling clarity, men and women arriving at La Colonia and being locked in a downstairs room. The Falange showed their only sign of humanity then. If anyone wished to confess, the parish priest of Víznar was summoned and heard them one by one, in a corner of the room, while upstairs the men who would kill them slept.

One story denied altogether that Lorca was taken to La Colonia, asserting that because of his status they kept him in a car parked somewhere in Víznar and then drove him to the house before dawn. Joaquín did not believe it. Other reports insisted on his incarceration in La Colonia where he spent the night with the local schoolmaster and five or six others. At dawn they were all herded outside and taken to the barranca where they were shot. Lorca was found lying beside the schoolmaster with a bright scarf loosely knotted around his neck, and it was also said that one of the gravediggers removed the scarf before he buried him.

Those were the facts he remembered as he stood there in the barranca, but they were only facts, abstract ciphers that merely outlined the tragedy which, for Joaquín, was cast in the colors of the dawn. The light would have been soft, he supposed, purple or red, and everyone, killers and victims alike, would have been shadowy presences on the path to the barranca from the old stone house. When the shots rang out in quick succession he imagined the birds which had nested in the trees flying up and away in a blur of wings, flying from death. He was so caught up in that vision that he scarcely noticed Bustamante uncorking the bottle.

"To Lorca and Lorenzo," he said, taking a long swallow. Then he handed the bottle to Joaquín who repeated the toast.

They passed the bottle back and forth until Joaquín suggested that they walk up the road. He wanted a better view of the place, more to remember. On the way Bustamante veered away toward La Colonia, saying that he wanted to be alone for a while.

Joaquín had known the visit would be painful, but he had no idea that the sight of the barranca would affect him so intensely. A weak breeze played through the olive trees. The cry of one bird sounded far away, emphasizing the silence as he reached the pool surrounded by feather-shaped leaves curling into dryness. Olive pits dotted the pale earth, and he stooped down and gathered up a handful. He was not in the habit of collecting mementos, but this was an exception. He put them carefully in his pocket and rose, remembering some of Lorca's poems. He forced himself to recite them because now the true nature of what had happened in the barranca was pressing in on him, breaking through his sadness, overriding the essentially sentimental thoughts and images with which he had protected himself from the moment he entered Bustamante's car. He was looking down into the barranca, reciting lines from the "Ballad of the Civil Guard" and "Romance Sonámbulo," anything that came to mind. He imagined the melody of a cante hondo such as Lorenzo might have sung, but neither poems nor songs could dull the image of Lorca lying there, hands trussed behind his back. He left the shade of Ainadamar then, strode quickly in the direction of La Colonia, but he always remembered that he turned away too late, failing to save himself from seeing Lorca sprawled in the barranca's dust where the rictus of death bloomed like blue flowers on his lyric lips.

They did not speak on the way back. Joaquín had paid close attention to everything from the moment they left the city hours earlier, but going to Fuente Grande was one thing, coming back quite another. They passed the cantina where the silent men had watched them through the beaded curtain. They passed the archbishop's palace. They went up and down the rises in Archbishop's Road, past the acequia, entered once again the vega that seemed much smaller now, and at each place Joaquín's outrage increased, as if the road from Fuente Grande to Granada were some contemporary Via Dolorosa, the cantina, palace, mountains and vega stations along the way speaking of an agony he no longer associated solely with Lorca but now with all of Spain. That morning, as he waited for Bustamante, he had read reports of the Nationalist atrocities. He read of supplies that had come into the hands of Franco's troops through the good offices of Germany and Italy. But it had taken his sojourn in the countryside to make it real, the sight of the barranca where Lorca's blood had so recently stained the earth, the intense memory of his passionate poems, to make him understand that what had been lost was merely the beginning. Spain was at risk in ways that had never seemed quite real until that moment. Lorca's death wounded his heart, but Fuente Grande wounded his conscience. By the time they reached Granada the shock of his stay in Berlin, the powerful but unfocused feelings that had come upon him in the railway station in Madrid—his dreaming uncle, his wound, his meeting with Lorca—were all swirling about in his mind, but it was not confusion he felt. He told me that it was one of those moments when the accumulated contradictions of a certain period of time suddenly coalesced in a single idea which expressed everything, condensed everything, froze the shifting shapes, clarified colors, focused images.

●

It was dark by the time they reached the hotel and Joaquín asked Bustamante to have dinner with him. The cabbie seemed to have anticipated the invitation. "It would be a pleasure," he said. "Do you want to eat here?"

"No. Take me where we can meet the right people."

"There will be some explaining to do, I mean about your passport. Other things. Spies are everywhere."

"Let me worry about that."

As soon as they entered the café called Los Tres Hombres Joaquín knew it was the place where Lorenzo had been arrested. A glance at Bustamante confirmed it.

"It is the best place to talk," Bustamante said, and then led him through the room to a table where five men looked at him with considerable surprise.

That night he met several rebel leaders. Nothing was said that might reveal what they did, even when Bustamante explained that Joaquín had been a friend of Lorca's. They ate and drank and Joaquín said that a sympathy grew among them that seemed even stronger because no one mentioned it. Nothing was resolved, but later, as he and Bustamante were about to leave, a man named Mendez, obviously the most influential of the five, told them to come back the following evening.

Need I insist on the obvious? Insist that Joaquín was only following the path of the golden thread that bound him and Lorca together in Madrid and even more closely in Fuente Grande? That the already complex twists and turns it had taken since he left his quiet, ordered life in Paris would become more intricate following that meeting with Bustamante's friends? What strikes me now as I try to follow its direction is how brightly it shone, how clearly the design moved through his days, how he gave himself up to a life that he later admitted to me had been unthinkable only a few months earlier.

The evening after he met Mendez he and Bustamante returned to the café and then went on to a small house in a poor section of the city. For the next week Joaquín, sometimes with Bustamante, sometimes with other members of the rebel group, met for long hours of questioning until Joaquín had satisfied their suspicions. It never occurred to him to stop and think about what he was committing himself to. Lorca's death had given him no choice. He joined the rebels and fought in several battles. He wrote communications, an activity which prepared the way later for another kind of writing in Paris which would lead him back to Spain, this time with me. I am certain he would have remained in Spain until the rebels were defeated if he had not accompanied a wounded friend to his home in Guernica.

José Ansaldo was a taciturn, retiring man, a carpenter by trade. Loyal as he was to his Basque homeland, Ansaldo had joined the rebels in the first weeks of the war. He and Joaquín met during a skirmish when they occupied the same position and were obliged to stay behind a farmhouse for several hours because of intense cross fire. It is no surprise that they formed a bond, and no surprise either that months later, when Ansaldo was wounded in the arm, that Joaquín would be worried enough to accompany his friend to his home.

He planned to spend a day or two with Ansaldo and his family, then make his way back to his unit. Ansaldo's wife, Gabriela, and their two daughters, María and Concepta, wept when they saw Joaquín and José coming up the street. Ansaldo's wound had opened during the trip, and as soon as he could Joaquín insisted on taking him to the hospital in Joséfinas where Ansaldo was put in a ward with several other militiamen.

Ansaldo was admitted late Sunday afternoon. Joaquín could have left then but Gabriela, who had apparently withstood her husband's absence bravely, dissolved into tears on the way back to the house. Joaquín decided to stay through Monday since that was market day in Guernica and he could help Gabriela bring back enough food to see the family through until she felt better.

He had gone to the market with her around noon and was helping her prepare dinner for the children when the bell in the church of Santa María rang. It meant nothing to him, but Gabriela dropped her knife and called to her daughters, who were playing outside.

"What is it?"

"The alarm for airplanes. We must go to the cellar."

He heard a plane coming in fast, the whistle of bombs, then a series of explosions near the station. María began whimpering, but Concepta ran to the window, even though her mother shouted at her to come back.

"Look, mother! They're so pretty!"

She was pointing to the sky where Joaquín saw three Junker bombers flying low over the town.

"Concepta," he shouted. "Do as your mother says!"

The little girl turned and looked at him reproachfully. "You're not my daddy."

That moment was etched into his mind for the rest of his life. Concepta was the picture of a beautiful, willful child. He admired her sense of herself, her defense of José's position in her life. Beyond her he saw the Junkers suddenly pull up, out of sight. He knew they had released their bombs and that they were all caught in that moment, as frozen in time as the people of Pompeii, weighted down by tons of ashes.

"Run for the cellar!" he shouted.

He had taken a step forward when everything turned white. Concepta, Gabriela and Mariá left their feet, flying toward him in a flutter of gaily-colored dresses.

He did not know where he was. He could not see or smell or

hear. His ears rang painfully and then there was a deeper sound, almost rhythmical, a pounding sound such as the heart makes sometimes in the ear when one is lying on a pillow. He listened to the sound. He said that that seemed all there was in life. He could not think. He doubted that he even knew who he was. His heart sounded big as a drum and then slowly the acrid smell of explosives came to him and soon the scent of wood smoke combined with the gunpowder. He was trapped in the rubble of Ansaldo's house. He tried to move but his left leg was pinned by a roof timber. His leg hurt and he knew it was broken as he called to Gabriela and the children. All he heard was the rhythm, the impossibly loud explosion of bombs and, when there was a pause, the vicious crackling of howling fires.

From his cave of rubble he could see much of the town. It was then he understood that he had been blown outside. He could not see a house standing. The only structure in his line of sight not destroyed by the rain of bombs was the Casa de Juntas where the old Parliament once sat. The branches of the famous oak of Guernica spread like black ganglia against the clouds reflecting the flaming town.

Guernica writhed in flames, but there were forms within them, unspeakable parodies of streets he had walked in only hours earlier that were now glowing heaps of red debris that bore no relation to the shapes of houses or other buildings. He looked at it, called again for Ansaldo's wife and children, lost consciousness. After a while he felt someone touching his face. He opened his eyes. Two men with cheeks blackened by smoke and soot were pulling him from the wreckage. He tried to speak but the only sound he managed was something like a croak. His throat ached and he went limp in their hands. Never in his life had he felt so helpless. The men cursed and pulled at the timber. When he was free they carried him to a cart.

He had no idea how long he had been trapped in the wreckage. All he knew was that the bombing had stopped, and that he was in the back of an old solid-wheeled farm cart drawn by oxen.

There were other people in the cart, though he did not know
how many, or whether they were men, or women, or children.
He hoped they were not children. He lay on his back, turning
his head left to right as they passed through the ruined town.
When the remains of buildings collapsed, huge waves of sparks
flew into the sky. He saw other carts piled high with household
possessions, government lorries filled with refugees. He had no
idea where they were going. He still could not think. The world
was reduced to various sensations of heat, multiple colors of fire,
flaming wooden frames of houses falling in upon themselves,
creaking wooden wheels of the cart that carried him and the
slower ones they sometimes passed. He heard cries, moans, the
ringing bells of fire brigades, and when these sounds receded,
when the light of the burning town dimmed, there was still
a reflection on the clouds. The procession moved through
Guernica slowly, and it seemed that a long time passed before
they entered into the countryside where farmhouses burned like
votive candles in the hills, little tents of flames rising up and
down against what he remembered vaguely of the look of things
when he and Ansaldo reached the town the day before.

By that time he had grown feverish. His leg ached, his head
ached. He struggled to stay awake, to attend to what was happening. The men on the seat encouraged the oxen. From time to
time he heard them talking, but there was no order to their
words. They said people had been machine-gunned as they ran
into the fields. "No," one said, "impossible." "Look!" the other
said. "The sheep. They killed all the sheep." Their voices mingled with other conversations. He heard his aunt, Lorca, Ansaldo
on the train. "Look, mother," Concepta said. "They're so
pretty."

He woke to the scents of bandages, of iodine and plaster of
Paris. His eyes were swollen, though he did not know it until he
tried to see. His eyelids felt stretched, lacerated, but he forced
them open because he was suddenly afraid of the redness. He
stared into a light fixture and for a moment fear seized him as he

mistook the bulb for an incandescent flame. Then he remembered the incendiary bombs he had seen from his cave. When he struggled to get up, a nurse with a harried expression put her hand on his chest and gently restrained him. He looked at her as she placed a finger to her lips. His leg was encased in plaster, elevated by some metal apparatus.

"You'll be fine," she said as she touched his forehead. Her hand was very cool. He could smell what he thought was a faint scent of perfume that mingled with the medicinal odors of the ward.

"Your leg's broken, but it isn't too serious."

"Where am I?"

"Bilbao. They brought you yesterday. You also have a concussion. Now, take this."

She helped him sit up and he swallowed the pills. Before lying back he saw that the ward was filled with bandaged, silent people.

"Sleep," she said.

He felt obedient as a child as he closed his eyes.

"Put your hand on my forehead," he asked, and he thought she stayed with him until he fell asleep.

He remained in Bilbao for two months. During the first week he was consumed by terrible pain in his head and leg. When it became so severe that he clutched at his temples a doctor gave him an injection of morphine.

"I can only do it when things are bad," the doctor said. "Supplies are very short."

He lived only in his pain that week. Never before had he felt so trapped in his body. Sometimes it seemed as though his body was Ansaldo's house and that he was nothing more than a network of nerve endings, of tiny blood vessels branching out like the filaments of a spider's web, like the old oak of Guernica. For a week he was nothing but pain and ganglia and he did not know if it was day or night.

When the pain subsided and he realized that he could think

again he sat up gingerly, afraid that some huge object would drop upon his head. It did not. He studied the ward, heard people moaning, heard the footsteps of doctors and nurses. His nurse approached. It seemed that he had known her long ago. She told him her name was Felicia.

"You're better," she smiled. "I knew it when I came in this morning."

"Tell me what happened."

She sat down. Reports were still coming in, she said, but it was clear that Guernica had been bombed and strafed with machine-gun fire for almost four hours.

"It's destroyed. No one knows how many people died."

The bald doctor with a mustache and goatee who gave him morphine approached and laid his clipboard on the table beside the bed. He took Joaquín's pulse and looked into his eyes with a small light. Then he stood up. Joaquín was thinking about what the nurse said. He saw Ansaldo's wife and children flying at him through the air and he had to tell the doctor and Felicia. He wanted to ask if they had heard anything, if any children were in the hospital, but he knew it was futile. He remembered how flames had engulfed the hospital where he had taken José.

"When can I go back?" he asked the doctor, and the man shook his head.

"The war is over for you. It's a serious break. You'll be able to walk on crutches with any luck in a few months, but I think you will never be able to run. And without running . . ." His voice trailed off and he made a clicking sound with his tongue. "We are grateful for everything."

Two months later Joaquín returned to Paris. St. Omer met him at the Gare d'Austerlitz where, over Joaquín's objections, he insisted on taking him to his own apartment until he no longer needed crutches.

Joaquín was relieved that his old friend refused to let him return home. He wanted someone to talk to, and he was also afraid of being alone. Every night his sleep was troubled by lurid images of flying children and the burning town. During the day he relived his trip to Guernica over and over. He knew that nothing he could have done in the town would have altered the outcome, but he had chosen to stay another day only partly because of the help he could offer Gabriela. The truth was that he had loved every minute away from the front. As soon as he and José had boarded the train and headed toward Basque country he felt safe for the first time in months. He deliberately decided to stay over to prolong the sense of safety, of normalcy, and now he could not avoid the guilt.

"It was cowardly. They needed every man they could find."

St. Omer looked at him in disbelief.

"You're full of shit, Wolf. Maybe there's still something wrong with your head. You gave them ten months." Then, pointing to his crutches, he added, "and your leg. This is romantic nonsense. You sound as if you'd only be satisfied if you died for Spain, or some such rot. If that's it, talk to someone else. A number of us regard you as remarkable, if that means anything to you."

St. Omer's words held no relief. As his friend talked, Joaquín was thinking of his fear, but most of all he thought of the dive-bombers approaching Ansaldo's house and how the swastikas on their fuselages shone brightly as the planes rose into the sky.

"I abandoned them. I should have gone back after I left José."

St. Omer understood what troubled him. There was no sarcasm in his voice when he said, "You'll feel better after a while."

He never did. Lorca's death, the fighting, the death of Ansaldo's family stained his soul like a birthmark. For the rest of his life he lived and wrote under the shadow of Guernica.

PART

2

CROSSING
November 26–December 13, 1942

3

W e met three years later, in the spring of 1940, after the
Nazis had taken over Czechoslovakia and Poland. No
one knew where it would end. Some of us thought France was
next, and much as I wished I did not have to think of Germany,
I was forced to by circumstances. Anxiety hung over Paris then
like fog, so thick you could almost touch it.

I remembered the feeling of that time yesterday when we
departed from Lisbon in a raging wind. I feel the same uncertainty about what lies beyond the horizon as I did when we
Parisians looked east, waiting for God knows what to appear.
Now of course there is a destination. The city of Los Angeles, a
district called Pacific Palisades. But I have no crystal ball, no
dice to cast whose numbers would tell the future. Everything is
in motion.

After waiting three and a half weeks I had begun to wonder if we'd ever leave. Every day Claude, Monika and I went to the harbor where the captain told dubious stories about provisions gone astray, problems with manifests, malfunctions of equipment as he calmly chewed the end of a dead cigar. With nothing but time on our hands, we explored a city for which none of us had an appetite. This is not to say that Lisbon lacked charm, only that its increasingly familiar streets and buildings and monuments were not quite real and served to remind us of Joaquín's absence. I was happy to see it disappear behind the rain.

After the interminable waiting I expected the crew would go about their business leisurely, but yesterday the captain and his mates were everywhere at once, barking orders and tearing their hair as if to make up for lost time.

So far as I can determine there are five other passengers besides ourselves, two couples and an elderly man. We nod politely when we meet, but everyone wants to keep to themselves. For the present I prefer it that way since I have quite enough company with Claude and Monika. Besides, I need the days to work. The captain said we will be at sea two weeks, longer if the weather's bad. Before I decided to try to make sense of what happened by writing, that would have seemed an eternity. Now I feel an urgency to get on with it and say what I can before we reach America.

Once we were settled I knew I couldn't spend my days in the cramped cabin I'd been assigned, so I have chosen this spot near the afterdeck of the ship. Already I have become accustomed to this watery world of the Mediterranean. Moreover, for an hour or two this morning, I enjoyed a certain celebrity. I had come on deck at first light with the idea of beginning my day as Joaquín used to do in Paris, when he was out in the streets at dawn searching for material. I'd started to write when members of the crew and one of the couples sauntered by to observe, quickly averting their eyes when I looked up. Their curiosity was soon satisfied, and now the men go about their business, having dismissed me as a harmless eccentric.

Yesterday, as I gripped the cold iron railing and watched Lisbon disappear behind the rain, I remembered Lorca's "Romance Sonámbulo" and saw our lives, Joaquín's and mine, replicated in its story. I told myself that people's lives don't follow the events in poems, yet ours did, his and mine. And so I thought, Since it's there, why not use it? Memory needs jogging into place. Otherwise it's only jumbled images and phrases seen like newspaper headlines out of the corner of the eye. So I will shape this against the background of that poem, looking at the sea the way the Gypsy looked over her balcony to the green pool below while she waited for her lover's return. I am well ahead of her in knowledge, seasoned with experiences that would have been quite beyond her, being the traditional Spanish woman that she was. Unlike her, I suffer no false hope, yet we are connected, this unnamed character in a poem and Ursula Krieger. Nowhere are we closer than when we contemplate the water and think of our men, hers a smuggler, mine a writer of some renown.

When I first read the poem I was lost in the lushness of its language so that only gradually, over a period of weeks, did the interior world of the Gypsy yield itself to my understanding. Now I have mastered it and can move from images to story, story to images. It is even easier here on the sea, whose greenness gives me the whole atmosphere wherever I look. I see her now on the sun-drenched plain, in her father's house with its flat roof and cistern pool. She loves a smuggler who rides on horseback across the hills to the sea where a ship bearing contraband comes to shore at night. His return is fraught with danger. Not only must he outwit the customs officers, but also the Guardia Civil, who are ordered to shoot such men on sight. She has waited for him night after night, leaning over the railing of the terrace where she stares at the all but invisible hills beyond the green weeds in the cistern. The light of the moon casts her face in a soft green glow. She is in love, obsessed, and soon her longing for him embraces sea, hills, wind until she conjures a green world that is cool and safe and without frustration. Enchanted, she throws herself into the pool, searching for him in the water, and as she sinks beneath the surface her lover, wounded by the Guardia, makes his way to her house, but she is dead when he arrives. Lying in bed, he hears the Guardia Civil at the door.

Thinking about it is like visiting a fortune-teller who tells me, "Look! Here is the path of your life. Lorca has set the path of her life upon yours, her lover's upon Joaquín's, the Guardia's upon the Guardia's!" But the fortune-teller's words are addressed to who I am now. Who I was requires sliding down the bright chute of memory, and I have hated memory for many years. Almost twenty years ago, when I held Monika with one hand and my box of money with the other, I moved us from Berlin to Paris with the single desire to kill the past. I pulled the blinds down in the train against her protests and those of two young men in our compartment. It was the first time she had ever been on a train. She wanted to see the countryside and towns, but I was finished with Germany and needed no more glimpses of Berlin's smoke-stained buildings, or quaint gingerbread villages gathered around church spires. In Paris I did my best to forget the Fatherland and succeeded except when my visitors arrived, those I came to call the Men in the Clock. When I drew the shades and bolted the door it did no good, for they entered despite my efforts, bearing my past on a silver platter.

Out here on the deck there is nothing to draw between me and the past, even if I desired it. A storm might blow in, but waves will never rise high enough to obscure Berlin. Clouds might graze the smokestacks, but there will always be an opening between clouds and sea, though it might be as narrow as the slits in glasses worn by Eskimos to protect them from the glare of snow. Childhood is already there behind the spiked helmets of the Kaiser's men bobbing along the streets like the sharp tips of iron fences. Behind them the house of childhood fronts a narrow street in a modest neighborhood far from Joaquín's family estate. In another world, actually. It was presided over by Mother's gentle, withdrawn spirit. I have never known anyone less demanding of life. A husband, children, enough food, a few flowers in the tiny plot she called her garden and she had reached the point of surfeit. You could see it in photographs taken at the time. A perfect cameo of a face framed by yellow hair, skin smooth as egg custard, eyes without guile, interest, or, sad to say, much intelligence. Mother reached the apogee of life at twenty-five, and balanced there like a ballerina frozen on point until my brother Jürgen died the day of his eleventh birthday. I hear the hushed voices and stifled sobs, see us gathered in the darkened parlor, Father bending over Mother who, until that moment, had sat straight in her chair, as if such stiffness could, like a charm, dispel the infection Father bent to tell her had killed her first-born child. She fell off point then, crumbled like a dusty rose.

The other clear memory I have of her was the way she polished the photographs of Jürgen which sat on her dressing table. Sometimes I saw her touching the tiny lips in the pictures, brushing back his shock of unruly hair. I remember Father standing over her six months after the funeral, hands by his side. He always stood that way, probably because it expressed his feeling of defeat. He remained perfectly still, but his voice rose as he told her that she could not bring him back, repeating it half a dozen times while she smiled at the photograph.

He and Mother were a pair in many ways. Most of all, I think, in the absence of ambition. They had found each other, and that was the major event in both their lives. They had produced me and Jürgen, and that gave them perfect contentment.

Father was a watchmaker by trade, and the intricate work had dimmed the larger world for him. Sometimes I went to his shop, which was hardly more than a hole in the wall on a long block of miscellaneous tradesmen. There I found a man unlike the one who returned home every night. With his jeweler's glass fitted into the socket of his left eye, he bent forward over his workbench with surprising energy and concentration. I thought there must be something wonderful in that tiny world of sprockets and gears, but when I begged to look through the glass I was disappointed. The mechanisms meant nothing to me, no more than abstract paintings do to many people.

The walls of his shop were lined with square and round and rectangular clocks ticking with a sound which, to my childish ears, seemed ominous. Even though I had no real conception of time, I became convinced that the walls of clocks were using it up, that there was only so much of it, and when they ran down something like the threat of doom I had to listen to every Sunday in our church would come upon us. They conjured evil, and I know that is why, many years later, I named my visitors the Men in the Clock.

But my visitors came much later, and I don't mean to dwell on the somber shade that seems to hover over my life so far. Childhood was an easy time for me and Jürgen. We were indulged, pampered, cosseted, spoiled. We were expert at throwing tantrums for which Mother weakly admonished us, setting up tiny, insignificant punishments. When Father returned, gazing blankly at us as she recounted the broken crockery, the pilfered sweet, the insolent language, a dreamy smile always came over his face as he called us to him and, looking at Mother, said, in his best imitation of authority, that we should be released. We learned the secret of our freedom early, and basked in it like birds in sunshine. I am convinced that Mother was relieved, too, for she probably looked forward to Father's assumption of supreme authority even more than we did.

Of Jürgen I can only say that he had the makings of a Teutonic warrior. In the castles he devised in the garden, or behind the sofa, he dictated to me the details of his imagined worlds. I was always the fair maiden kidnapped from her home, he the avenging minister of bloody justice, and it was not long before I tired of servitude. "But that's how it always is in books!" he'd cry. "I don't care," I'd answer, "you be the prisoner for a while and see how you like it." "That's for girls. Now pretend you're tied up in the dungeon."

When he died I was convinced he'd gone to hell, my vision of the afterlife having been effectively inculcated by our Lutheran minister. I looked at Mother and asked, "What is death?" and she broke into a fit of weeping so that Father had to take her into another room. When he returned I asked, "Will Jürgen go to hell?" "No, he's an angel now." He told me about the wonderful time Jürgen was having in a place where the streets were paved with gold. It wasn't hell, but I could not distinguish much between the freedom of heaven and the freedom Jürgen enjoyed on earth. I asked what the difference was and, confounded, Father took me by the hand and led me to my aunt, saying that he had work to do and I should ask her about such things.

I suppose his passivity made it inevitable that I would be drawn to someone utterly unlike him. It wasn't conscious or deliberate. At sixteen I was attracted to a boy in school who was impossibly handsome and wrote poems. He always won the prize, and when he read his work in class—it was exclusively medieval and reminded me of my castle life with Jürgen—I wanted him to rescue me. But another girl struck his fancy and I was miserable for weeks.

Not long afterward I met Hans. I was out of school and, since Father's business was failing, there was no money for further education. I'd found a job in a millinery shop, and one day Hans came in looking for a piece of fine cloth to give his mother. He was only a year older than me, but he seemed to come from another world. His blond hair was closely cropped, his mustache full, and he was handsome in a grown-up way. What appealed to me was his sense of purpose and the vigor of his speech, which was so unlike Father's whisper.

He had lived in Munich for a while, but the position had not worked out and he had joined the army. The next time I saw him he was resplendent in his uniform. He asked me to walk in the park one Sunday, and other invitations followed. One night —it was summer and we had gone to the circus and walked back through the park—he drew me in under the trees. I knew what he wanted, and I was suddenly as eager as he was when he parted my thighs. The pain did not matter. It was an adventure and I loved him. When I asked if he had taken precautions I felt his heart beating as he said no and pulled away. "I'm sorry," he said, "I'm sorry," and I told him there was nothing to be sorry for.

Two months later I had to tell him I was pregnant. We were having dinner that night in a restaurant. After the waiter brought coffee I reached across the table and touched his arm. "There's something you need to know. I'm going to have a baby."

He stiffened, not dramatically, not comically either. He just sat up rigidly in his chair, touched his tie and straightened his lapel as if he were going on parade. Since leaving the doctor's office I'd been consumed by dozens of thoughts, chiefly the awareness that my life had changed irrevocably. That was what I saw in his face too, as well as a feeling of entrapment.

"Well," he said finally in a pinched voice, "we must marry."

"I'm not asking for that," I answered, though God only knows what I'd thought I'd do by myself. All I remember is that it seemed terribly important, and not a little noble, to give him that option. I suppose I was also interested in seeing how he would respond, and it was the only time in our life together that he ever disappointed me. I saw him stray away at that point. He had his moment of loss when he saw his freedom flying out the window, but I could not begrudge him that. I'd felt exactly the same only hours earlier.

"We wanted a child," I said.

"We did." In the same breath he called to the waiter for champagne.

It seemed as if my life had found direction. I have often looked back to that time, trying to see who I would have been if the Great War had not intervened. I would surely have been a different woman. My God, yes! A stranger. And would I have liked her, this other Ursula? I remember a story where a character confronts the person he might have been at the top of a staircase. *Mon semblable, mon frère* indeed! *Ma soeur, mon enfant* more likely, for how could she have been anything other than a child, a naïf? I would likely have lived my life out as Mother did hers, had more children, poured endless cups of tea and made tons of rouladen for Hans's superiors in various posts until, gray-haired and serene with Mother's numbness, I would have been the commander's wife and counseled young women who came to my house in the protocols of military life.

But there was no other Ursula. I was formed by these memories and voices:

Father's, for instance, a few months after Mother died, his sweet dreamy smile intact at the crest of a double defeat. "The business failed. I've sold the stock, but there's hardly enough to get by on for a year. I know Hans's salary isn't large . . ." And how, every few weeks, I would send him something.

Hans's, soon after Franz Ferdinand's assassination, the first week of the war. "Our unit has been called. You'll be fine." His going down the walk in his dress uniform like a businessman off for a day at the office.

One month later to the day, the voices of two officers: "We regret . . ." Monika tugging at my hand, wanting to know who they were, friends of Papa's?

After Hans died I scarcely felt any connection with the world. I seemed to float over Berlin as the war raged on and our lives became poorer and more confined from day to day. Monika and I survived frugally as birds in winter while I scratched out a meager living doing chores for those more fortunate. The fighting ended with the Armistice, but we were even more impoverished then. I was ignorant of the causes. All I knew was that the war years seemed like a time of abundance, for what I earned could not sustain us any longer. No matter that I labored twelve and sometimes fifteen hours washing and cleaning. My money bought less and less, and soon there was no work at all.

Poverty gnaws at the body before it feasts on the mind. At least that was the case with me. Perhaps it was pride, the simple refusal to acknowledge defeat. I trained my body to accept less food, giving Monika every scrap I could, but it was not enough. She grew thinner from the time I put her to bed at night until the next morning when her shoulders and spindly legs appeared more gaunt. She developed a dry, hacking cough that my home-made nostrums could not cure. One day, as I watched her devouring a crust of bread, a day when I had no work of any kind, I was reminded of Hans, for she had his coloring, his mouth and nose, and it seemed that I was losing him again because I suddenly understood that she might also die. At that moment our poverty entered my mind in the image of dark semicircles that had appeared beneath her eyes. She is starving, my mind said. She is going to die unless you do something. I have never experienced a greater moment of clarity, a more profound moment of insight, than I did as I looked at Monika's transparent face. Everyone has one experience that sets its seal upon them, becomes the watershed by which all other events are judged. Until that morning I had thought it was Hans's death, my young, untimely widowhood, but that was only the prelude to the walk I took that night.

•

In those years after the war Berlin danced crazily in ruin, hanging his shaggy head in defeat one moment, his ponderous feet shuffling unsteadily as an aged derelict's; then, in the next, he spun wildly, laughing, leering, leaping in the air with frenzied dexterity, ignorant both of what he mourned and thought he celebrated.

On certain days old Berlin rose phoenixlike above the bitter ashes of his defeat, stretching his abundant arms wide enough to embrace the grossest contradictions that had come upon him. He seemed to say, with a great old-fashioned voice, that he could conquer this affliction and implored us to be patient, to wait for another flowering of his soul. But the bluster and promises could not conceal his ruin, his masklike face, the false bravado in his voice. Oh, there were some who, through luck or graft or guile found it possible to believe his promises, but for most of us it was only a matter of time before we understood that we were locked in a charlatan's embrace.

After defeat shredded his finery I walked in his shadow, looking for the simplest necessities, trying, without success, to discover how Monika and I might survive. I ironed, washed, cleaned, but the money dropped into my hands at the end of those long days could not withstand the inflation that rendered it almost worthless from the time my employers opened their purses until my fingers closed gratefully over those greasy coins.

And so one evening I asked my neighbor, Frau Baumgarten, an old Prussian who lived on a bowl or two of watery gruel each day, if she would stay with Monika that night in exchange for a few of my worthless coins. She did not even ask how many, agreeing immediately and saying that she always thought Monika was the prettiest child in the building. Nor did she ask where I was going, but only looked at me with a kind of pity and understanding, and then I knew that she knew.

That night I put on my best dress, rouged my cheeks, made myself attractive. I walked for blocks in the shadow of old Berlin. When my courage failed I backtracked, went down alleys, stopped outside cafés I could not afford to enter, but there was always movement because there had to be, and so I made my way through the reeling city, through decrepit squares and under elegant arching trees until I reached the street where I saw the sign of the Seven Dolphins, passing beneath it without a second glance as I entered a dimly lighted salon where a dozen women plied their trade.

The madam was a stately redhead who called herself Odile. She wore a green sequined dress that made her look like an emerald obelisk topped with fire. Her eyes were green too, as was the mascara that made them into a mask. The only thing that spoiled her beauty was the pockmarks on her cheeks, which even heavy makeup did not conceal. She stood with her ringed hands on her hips as I stammered out why I'd come, looking me up and down with the same rudeness I sometimes encountered from men passing on the street. Then she pursed her lips, nodded, and told me to come into her office, a small room off the salon which was filled with antiques and was as proper as the sitting room of a maiden aunt. She poured two schnapps from a crystal decanter and drank hers off like a sailor. She twisted the glass between her fingers and stepped to the side, examining me as if I were on display in a shop window. Finally she put the glass down on the bar.

"You know what you're getting into?"

I said yes.

"You won't complain if you don't like a customer? The rule is that you take what comes in the door."

"I need the money," I answered. "This is the only way I can see."

I spoke as confidently as I could, trying to match her frankness, though what I said made me dizzy with fear and disgust.

"Well," she said, pursing her lips, "I could use another girl tonight."

"Tonight?"

"If not you, someone else," she said impatiently. "They come in all the time now, three or four a night, and with less compunction. So?"

I asked what she wanted me to do.

"Take off your clothes. I need to see if anything's wrong. Sometimes there are birthmarks, moles. I offer only clean bodies. Don't worry," she added, "I'm not that way."

I undressed down to my underclothes.

"Everything."

When I stood before her naked she nodded.

"Very nice. A little thin, but you'll be popular. Wait a minute."

She turned away, rummaged through a wardrobe, and handed me a red and black chemise.

"You can wear this the first week. After that I expect all my girls to buy their own. Talk to the others. They'll tell you where to go."

Then she smiled for the first time. "Haven't you forgotten something?"

"What?"

"You haven't asked about the money. Don't feel bad. It happens with girls who haven't been in the life."

I had no idea what to expect. She told me what the fees were for an hour, two hours, the whole night.

"You take the money before you go upstairs and give it to me. I pay your percentage when you're ready to leave."

It was more than I'd hoped for. As I stood there listening to Odile I did quick calculations in my head. If I were frugal there would be enough to save.

"Come. We'll be busy soon."

I followed her to the salon as if I were walking into a dream. A dozen other women dressed more or less as I was were talking to a few men or lounging on black sofas. When I saw them I felt degraded and soiled but I put my feelings away, carefully and consciously locked them up even as Odile introduced me. That was the only way I could endure what was coming.

The men moved among us, choosing their pleasures like connoisseurs. I did not know what I was supposed to do so I stood there, in the middle of the room, looking away whenever someone glanced in my direction. A man sat down beside the young blond woman on the sofa. I could not believe my eyes when he slipped his hand between her thighs, which parted abruptly, like obedient fish. Another man with uncertain eyes asked my name. I smelled liquor on his breath.

"Ursula," I replied, "Ursula Krieger," but my name had no connection with me. When I felt his hand on my breast I closed my eyes, telling myself that this body was only something I would use to feed Monika, it was not me. He was smiling when I opened them.

"You like that, don't you?"

As he took some bills from a wallet I translated them into a pot of stew filled with large, fatty chunks of meat, with cabbage and carrots and turnips. I imagined filling a bowl for Monika, watching her eat.

After that night my life followed a rigid pattern. When I returned home at three or four in the morning I deposited my earnings in a metal box on the floor of a closet. Then I woke Frau Baumgarten, paid her, walked her to the door. We rarely spoke because we had nothing to say. For each of us there was only necessity. My choice made it possible to survive. Speech under such conditions would have been obscene, so we parted silently, usually without even looking at each other, until the following night.

After closing the door I went into the room where Monika slept, made sure she was covered, then returned to the kitchen where I brought two kettles of water to boil on the stove, poured them into the bathtub, washed. I lay in the tub until the tepid water went cold because the bath afforded a kind of sanctuary— it was my own place. When it grew too cold I put on a robe and sat on the sagging bed. I had no dressing table, only a scarred chair on which to balance a tortoiseshell mirror. I adjusted the lamp until it shone on my face, saw how the harsh light made my complexion white as winter. My face was hardening into a mask, and I sometimes thought that it had grown so thin I could push my hand through it if I tried.

Then I began combing. My hair was long in those days, deep blond, no traces of gray. In this combing I was like hundreds of other women in Berlin. Some went through the ritual automatically, or sleepily, or lovingly watching themselves, admiring the face in the mirror, the sheen of their hair, perhaps playing coquettishly to a husband or lover standing in the shadows or lying on a bed anticipating the pleasures that were coming.

There are many ways women comb their hair, many motives, but none matched mine as I tilted the lampshade until the light shone on my face and hair. There was a contrast between my dull, almost transparent skin and the highlights of my hair, which was burnished by combing, gleaming with silver, undulating like lazy waves. I combed slowly, deliberately, combed out kisses, caresses, the scents of beer and wine and schnapps, of uniforms and starched collars and workingmen's shirts. I watched the comb moving through my hair, and with each rhythmical movement forced myself away from the Seven Dolphins, forced myself to think only of the money accumulating, soiled bill by soiled bill in the metal box, to hear nothing but the faint susurrus of the comb, which lulled me as if it were the sound of the sea.

For the first few weeks at the Seven Dolphins I entertained the illusion that I was an outsider, telling myself that what brought me there made me different from the others. They quickly sensed my aloofness and soon ignored me. The silence was not broken until one night when I suddenly began crying. I tried to get hold of myself by asking Elsie if she understood the meaning of the Seven Dolphins. She shrugged and told me to ask Odile, who had just come in. When Odile saw me crying she said, "Come with me," and, taking me firmly by the arm, led me into her office. She poured a drink for herself and then looked at me with that peculiar way of hers as she pursed her lips.

"I have no time for nonsense, Ursula. It's up to you. I have no trouble finding girls, not at all. You'll make no money this way, and it creates a bad impression. You don't need to laugh— some of them like it when you're moody—but you can't cry. No one wants a weeper. It makes them feel guilty. I'll give you another night, but only one. Understand?"

I was too distraught to bathe when I got home. I had wept on the way back, and when I looked in the mirror my face was trapped behind bars of wet mascara. There was nothing to do. Leaving the Seven Dolphins was out of the question. It was a matter of how to endure, separate myself from what I saw in the mirror. I tried thinking of happier times but always I saw the salon, the women, the men, the tiny rooms upstairs. The clearest image of all was the sign over the entrance, lighted by a naked bulb. Words in white script hovered over a black sea where gray dolphins moved from left to right, floating on the surface, their shapes hardly distinguishable from the murky water.

That was the first night my visitors spoke. Over the previous few weeks my clients' faces sometimes appeared to me during the day. Monika and I might be in a park, or talking at lunch, and suddenly one of them was there, his face clear as a photograph superimposed on a swath of grass, a wall, my daughter's face. I felt a sudden surge of guilt and disgust, especially if I was looking at Monika when it happened. I'd turn away, force myself to think of something very specific like a window in a building, the shape of a tree, a picture in the apartment. The face would vanish then and I'd struggle to regain my balance, hurrying away from the park, or quickly open one of Monika's books of fairy tales and read to her with as much animation as I could manage.

Something changed that night. Maybe it was because I couldn't avoid thinking about the sign, or that I was exhausted. It doesn't matter. All I knew was that I had no resistance left, no stores of energy. I seemed to be looking through those black bars that streaked my face at half a dozen men I'd entertained. They had a maddening tendency to change shapes, appearing in two or three different manifestations within seconds. Sometimes they were merely men, like strangers one sees in the street. At others their features resembled gargoyles perched on buttresses and eaves of churches. Then they settled into the shapes of figures who parade on revolving platforms of clock towers. I would have laughed at the crudity of my imagination if I hadn't been so frightened. The clock was the perfect symbol of my nights at the Seven Dolphins where my clients and I went up the stairs to join in whatever embrace they desired for the time Odile so carefully prescribed. The Men in the Clock I said to myself, and they all smiled the moment that I named them.

I was on the verge of despair. One of them, a soldier named Kurt who always chose me, seemed to be carrying my metal box. He rattled it and the coins inside jangled obscenely. He held the box out, as if he were showing it to me. "Remember," he said. "Remember your bargain, Ursula. Can you hear yourself?" He held the box up to his ear and rattled it. "I hear you." Then he laughed. "The sound of Ursula Krieger, no?"

A week later, as I lay in my bath, they came again, this time parading around the old porcelain tub, their footsteps making the floor creak like the stairs at the Seven Dolphins. They looked down at my nakedness and even though I turned on my side and crossed my arm over my breasts I felt totally exposed to their leering eyes. I was nothing but that pale white body, an instrument, a vessel for their pleasures. I was empty as my womb, a hollow gourd with no identity other than my function. I was approaching nothingness, I was only a darkness to be filled over and over with Odile's voice, men's voices, their penises as they groaned and whispered obscenities into my ear. I did not think I could abide that darkness another moment, nor the blackness of the sea, nor the endless repetition of the dolphins' turgid swimming. I was falling through the darkness, engulfed by tepid water, sinking into it when the man in the apartment next to mine began playing his piano.

I knew nothing about him, not even his name. He had arrived a few months earlier with a battered suitcase. I saw him as I came upstairs that day, and even though he must have sensed my presence, he neither turned nor paused but went right on in and slammed the door.

The next day I heard a commotion on the stairs, opened the door and saw him with another man in equally tattered clothes carrying the tiniest piano I had ever seen. Even then it was a struggle. They sweated, cursed and finally laughed when they reached our landing. The piano had wheels which allowed them to push it into his apartment.

I had no idea what to expect. He was thin as a reed and his hands appeared to shake. It occurred to me that he might very well be a drunken musician such as the one who played popular songs in the parlor of the Seven Dolphins. If that had been the case I do not know what I would have done. The music sickened me. Its jangling rhythms and lewd lyrics would have meant no respite at all from my employment. In my hours of freedom I would have to listen as he played and sang, as if my life with Monika were merely a prelude to what I did at night.

I prepared myself for the worst, but it was not necessary. Not a sound came from my neighbor's apartment for over a week. When it did it was Debussy, and not the way an amateur would play him.

He had a repertoire of a dozen pieces, mostly etudes. Sometimes he played them all, one after the other, over a period of several hours. The duration seemed limited by perfection, for as soon as he made a mistake there would be a crashing discord he could only have made by smashing his arm across the keyboard, followed by curses and shouts of self-loathing. But this happened rarely. Most of the time he performed with a lovely, muted elegance that transformed the music on that tinny, out-of-tune instrument into something serene and fine.

That night he played *La Mer*, making its melody ethereal and sensuous. It stopped my sense of falling, of being engulfed by the dark water of the sign. It seemed to me that he had never played so well, and I gratefully gave myself up to the music, let it wash over me as I lay back and closed my eyes. I still saw the sign but it no longer threatened me. *La Mer* had somehow interposed itself like a protective shield. The water was lighter now, aquamarine, the color of Mediterranean coves. I forced myself to enter. It was a conscious, deliberate act of mind, a conjuring of water, coolness, color.

There, in that cove in my mind, the gray dolphins of the sign circled in the distance, their fins no different from those of sharks. I could feel the dream or the illusion or the hope—I scarcely know what to call it even now—breaking, giving way to the despair I could not cope with, when I saw the first white dolphin, and in that instant the grays disappeared, vanishing without a trace.

The dolphin swam to me, circled me, eyed me, its movements perfectly synchronized with the rhythms of *La Mer*. Another appeared, then another until there were seven. They were there because of the music, coming closer because of the music, and I remembered the crashing of my neighbor's arm across the keys, hoped that he would not miss a note.

I wondered what they wanted from me. I questioned the nearest one who answered with a clicking sound, a pleasant staccato rhythm that held no words but seemed to say they wanted nothing, that it was my need they had come to fulfill.

And then I joined them, moved with them, swam in the cove in perfect time to Debussy. We turned away from the narrow opening of the cove and headed toward open sea. They arched above the surface, and as I swam among them I surrendered my body, was one more white form in that green-blue sea, a leaping, dancing creature revealing her whiteness to the sun only, saying in watery whispers that never, never had I been anything but this. Never anything but this free white form, unconstrained and inviolable.

Night after night I entered those green waters. Night after

night I left the salon with my patrons and climbed the stairs to the narrow rooms where I endured whatever they had paid for. But in my mind I never stayed. Whether the lights remained on, or were extinguished by an impatient hand, I continued up and up, through the shingled roof, out into the night where I found the warm green sea. Night after night, as I added to the hoard of money in my metal box, week after week, as Monika's spindly arms and legs grew firm, her face ruddy with new health, I lived among white dolphins.

•

There has been some progress, enough pages are filled to give this diary bulk and me some satisfaction. I am almost tempted to claim the status of a playwright and see this wind-swept deck as an impromptu stage where the principal actors in my life stand about sipping coffee and gossiping as they wait impatiently for the curtain to go up again. But the comparison is too simple because it suggests a clarity of understanding. The truth lies closer to the work of a cartographer tentatively map-ping the districts of her life, which have yet to coalesce into a whole.

The ship groans and creaks. A veil of clouds, all that's left of yesterday's storm, floats to leeward where the sea unfolds like parchment and the line of my life connects Berlin to the Somme, Berlin to Paris, Paris to Spain and Portugal. The route to Hans is short and stops abruptly, the one from my apartment to the Seven Dolphins black as the anguished stroke of a dis-traught painter. The map shows an angry line running from my beginnings to Hans, Monika, the Men in the Clock. Tomorrow I will begin the road to Joaquín. It will be circuitous, tentative, unsure of itself at first, a meandering route edged with hesita-tions and doubts, but it will gather strength as it winds through the City of Light and becomes entwined with two other men.

o

The map is incomplete without them, its terrain scarcely recognizable until I have laid in the lines to Gerhard Munch, who followed my thoughts back to Berlin, and Guy Lafont, who believed Joaquín was his salvation.

4

A few months after returning from Bilbao Joaquín was out in the streets of Paris, hobbling about on a cane. One day he found himself in the lower reaches of Montmartre where he discovered a café called La Masia tucked away on a narrow street. From the outside it seemed little more than a hole in the wall, scarcely different from other cafés in the district. The tables on the sidewalk were occupied by old men in jackets and berets who nursed drinks and followed the sun like so many pale flowers. But inside it was Spain. A dozen tables were crowded together in two rows, and in the back there was a table suitable for banquets. A zinc bar ran the length of one wall with a discolored mirror against which shelves displayed an array of sherries. Bullfight posters hung close together on all the walls, each celebrating a torero who had died on the horns of the bulls in the gaudy drawings or retired long before Joaquín happened to stop there.

La Masia reminded him immediately of Los Tres Hombres in Granada. He soon became a regular and struck up a friendship with Rodríguez, the owner, who could not do enough for him once he learned that he had found against Franco. During the next few months Joaquín brought his friends to La Masia, which gradually became a gathering place for literary people, a kind of informal salon that met irregularly for discussions and readings from their work and that of others they admired. A pleasant anarchy reigned, and while they shouted and insulted each other, they settled into La Masia and became something of an institution.

Besides their literary concerns they were a fiercely political group, arguing endlessly over the news from Spain and Germany. Lorca's murder was still fresh in their minds, and it was not surprising that one day, encouraged by Joaquín, they agreed to name themselves in Lorca's honor. Ricard, who was a part-time sculptor, volunteered to make a small plaque with his name on it and the dates of his life. A month later he finished a bronze casting with THE LORCA CLUB inscribed in thick raised letters. Rodríguez made a great show of accepting it in the name of all Spaniards. Then he excused himself and returned from the back with a drill, made holes in the wall, and screwed the plaque to it. He told one of the waiters to bring two bottles of good cognac. Everyone stood with full glasses while Sandoz proposed a toast. St. Omer asked Joaquín to say a few words. He told them about meeting Lorca, described his hand raised in farewell beneath the streetlight, recalled what he said about the rain. He wondered if Lorca had known it was bearing down even then, if he had known that the Guardia who taunted him as he went along the street presaged what happened at Fuente Grande. While he spoke it seemed as if he heard the shot that killed Lorca as clearly as the clink of glasses set down upon the table, as if the bullet had not died with him, had not buried itself in the rocky soil of Fuente Grande but took flight, arching over Víznar, rising above the Pyrénées, above Spain and France until it fell, spent but shining, on the banquet table at La Masia.

It happened that Claude was there that day because St. Omer had recently taken him in hand and decided to introduce him to the group. He had been publishing reviews that were so exceptional he'd been asked to contribute regularly to several important papers. An editor invited him to his apartment on the Ile de la Cité where he met St. Omer, a happy piece of luck since Claude had begun to think that the literary life of Paris was inaccessible to him because he did not write imaginatively.

That had not always been the case. When he was younger he wrote poetry and continued after he began his academic career, though by then he'd begun to feel it was all in vain. One day he looked through the stack of rejection notices he'd received and realized quite suddenly that he would never write anything publishable. He emptied his folders into the fireplace, expecting a few minutes of satisfying self-pity. Instead there was only relief, and that saved him from months of brooding over his defeated hopes. He threw himself into teaching, transferring the passion he'd brought to his poetry to his lectures as he paced back and forth with all the conviction of a fundamentalist preacher trying to coax belief from a skeptical flock. Soon students poured into his classes. Young men imitated his speech and mannerisms, and some women regarded him with more than the light of literary interest in their eyes. Monika was one of them.

He was puzzled by her at first. Her remarks were always perceptive, but she made them offhandedly, almost always with a sense of humor. Once he asked why she read only some of the works he assigned. She laughed and said it wasn't his fault. She wanted to become a photographer, and read only those things she thought might be useful in sharpening her eye.

One rainy afternoon he proposed a drink. It was indiscreet but he could not help himself. She was wearing a black sweater and skirt, and during his lecture he could not keep his eyes off her. As soon as they sat down in the café their legs touched and it was all over for him then. He was already thinking about when he could see her again. She encouraged him by saying that she often thought about what he said in class while she worked in a bakery every afternoon. That explained what had, until then, been one of her mysteries. He had noticed the scent of bread the first time they met, and its effect was as erotic as perfume. When he got home that night he held a slice of bread to his nose. Never had anything smelled so clean and fresh.

I knew she had a lover, but it was several months before she brought him home. When she did there were things I had to say. After tea she took the cups and dishes into the kitchen, leaving us alone. I'm afraid I confronted him without any warning. "Monika is a grown woman," I said, "but you must forgive me for exercising a mother's privilege. I know you're sleeping together. It's been obvious for some time. I'd like to know what you want."

He was caught off guard. He knew where the conversation was heading, and I remember him looking at the closed kitchen door, obviously hoping that Monika would come in and save him. When she didn't, the best he could do was to say lamely that he loved her.

"Ah, love," I answered with a wave of the hand. "The word comes easily at this point. I would like to know what lies beyond it, what you want with her. I only ask that you respect her. She admires you for what you are, but it's easy for young women to mistake admiration for other things. She can have sex with anyone, but she needs more than that. I ask that if you don't want her, you give her up. You're handsome, and would have no trouble finding someone else."

It was difficult saying those things, but I had no choice, even if it occasioned a fight with Monika. It wasn't possessiveness that forced my little catechism, but a need to protect her. The Seven Dolphins had taught me things I didn't want to know.

While I knew that all men weren't like those who frequented the parlor there, I was skeptical about men, wary as an animal when it senses danger to its young.

But there was nothing to fear from Claude. They married a year later, and we all went to live in an apartment on the Rue de Seine, where I found a larger life for myself tutoring neighborhood children most afternoons. The money helped with expenses, but that was less important than the opportunity it afforded. Monika's youth had been speeded up by the war, Hans's death, our poverty. Although I was not at fault, we had been deprived of her childhood. There was nothing I could do for her now, but there was the tutoring for me. Children who were slow learners, children who were brilliant, children who were wealthy and very poor studied with me. The lessons were for half an hour, but I always arranged for the strugglers to come early. I sympathized, teased, scolded, mothered, did whatever was necessary, and I succeeded.

•

Claude knew I was intrigued by *Dawn* and *Morning*. In fact, we had discussed them only a few days after St. Omer took him to La Masia. He had found Joaquín charming, and had been deeply moved by his eulogy to Lorca. It happened that he was preparing an article on Parisian novelists at the time, and asked me to look at his first draft. I agreed with his assessment of Joaquín's talent, but it seemed to me he'd glossed over an aspect of the work I found unsettling. The novels had a peculiar sense of distance and made me feel as if I were wandering rather aimlessly in a gallery filled with beautiful pictures. Everything was rendered with great precision, but the overall impression was stark and unforgiving. I remember telling Claude I felt a certain disjunction between the quality of the writing and Heinz's austere point of view. I think I even mentioned a sense of doubleness, a conflict, as if there were two warring perceptions at work.

"I agree," he said. "He seemed different at the club, quite passionate. But what the devil, Ursula, this is what he's chosen to write."

He reminded me of the Preface to *Dawn* where Joaquín laid out his theory, claiming that his purpose was merely to record the totality of Parisian life in what he hoped would be the equivalent of a series of black and white photographs. Heinz was to be a wandering eye, a system of observation.

The more we talked the more I realized I wasn't such a fan of Joaquín Wolf as I supposed. Something was missing. I was uneasy about the novels' disengagement, and all the more puzzled by Joaquín's apparently passionate speech at the Lorca Club. The two didn't go together.

One Friday, a few weeks later, Monika spent longer than usual shopping. Though it seemed odd, I said nothing until Sunday morning when they began packing a picnic hamper. They were acting strangely and I finally put down my book and demanded to know what was happening.

"You two act like conspirators."

Monika laughed and Claude fought to keep a straight face.

"Tell me. You know I don't like surprises."

Claude was on the verge of giving it away when there was a knock at the door.

"That's the reason. We have a guest."

"Who?"

"Someone you'll like."

Monika opened the door before he could say anything else.

"Mein Gott!" I said. I recognized Joaquín immediately from photographs in the papers. The exclamation made me feel rude and unsophisticated. Most of all, it embarrassed me. I had mastered French well enough to think in it easily, but whenever something unexpected happened a German phrase tended to catch me unawares.

○

Much later Joaquín told me that he noticed my startled expression when Monika opened the door. It dominated me entirely so that for a moment that was all I was, a startled woman. Only after I gained control of myself did I come into focus. He knew I was Monika's mother. We had the same cheekbones, the same eyes, the same shoulders. I remember that my surprise faded into a kind of apology in the way I said, in my best French, that I was happy to meet him.

"It's my pleasure," he said in German, adding that he recognized a Berlin accent and asked if I was raised there. I cursed myself. I felt trapped by his question, led in a direction I did not want to take. When I answered there was a certain brittleness in my voice.

"I was there until a little after the war."

He asked what part of the city I lived in. I wanted to lie. I was willing to say anything, but when I tried to remember names of other districts and streets my mind went blank. He was standing there, waiting for an answer, and I was so confused by his unexpected question that I mentioned the place where I lived, as well as the street where the Seven Dolphins was. I could not believe it and tried to cover my mistake by saying that I had worked there for a while in a café.

"It was not pleasant," I added, "but then nothing was after the war."

I remember turning the question on him, asking about his past. He told me where his family lived, and that he had been in Paris ten years, adding that it seemed like all his life. Claude had brought some wine and he stood there beside me, speaking up only when it seemed we might lapse into silence. He knew that inviting Joaquín had been risky because there was no way to predict how I would respond. Now he was pleased. Except for that moment of uncertainty he was convinced that I was too. It was quite remarkable. I can't say exactly why, but I felt better than I had in months, and the feeling only became more pronounced as we went out to the Bois de Boulogne on the métro. I felt free. My years in Paris had been spent making a shock-proof life. Now I found myself in an unpredictable situation and, for the first time in years, I did not care. That, too, came as a surprise.

The park was crowded with people enjoying the warm spring day. I was struck by the idea that it seemed perfectly normal to be there with Joaquín Wolf, though I had no illusions about the situation. I had trained myself to expect nothing. It was the guiding principle of my life and I told myself that this was only a momentary respite.

We found a place beneath a tree within sight of the pond, put down blankets, removed the food and wine. As we ate, Monika tore the crusts from her bread and insisted we do the same, saying that she wanted to feed the swans. After we finished the apple tarts and sauternes she stood up, smoothed her skirt, and took Claude's hand.

"Come on," she said. "It's their turn. I saved some of my tart in the event one of them has a sweet tooth."

As they left Joaquín turned to me. "She is really quite charming. You must be proud."

It was warm even in the shade of the tree. The four of us had finished two and a half bottles of wine and I felt quite relaxed. I was sitting up, resting my weight on my hands. Joaquín lay on his side. He had taken off his hat and his hair looked grayer in the mottled light. It was then that I saw the scar with the peculiar shape. Monika and Claude were squatting down at the water's edge, tossing bread to the swans. People strolling by cast interested glances at me and Joaquín. I knew they assumed a relationship, and the notion of such a connection startled me. It was so inappropriate, and I was afraid that he might intuit what I was thinking.

I blushed. I couldn't help it. It was an old affliction, and most of the time I could stop it by talking, but that was another problem because I felt unaccountably shy. I was almost fifty, hardly an age when one ought to suffer from girlish inhibitions. I

wanted Claude and Monika to come back because it had been
easier to talk to Joaquín with them present, but they had gotten
up and wandered farther away so I tried to cover my confusion
by tidying up the dishes. Joaquín helped, and there was a brief
respite as we collected plates and glasses and silverware. I knew
he was waiting for me to speak, but my mind was blank until I
remembered that Claude had met him the day the Lorca Club
was formed. I asked him about it, adding, "He must have meant
a good deal to you—Lorca, I mean."

He said yes, that was true. As soon as I mentioned Lorca's
name he withdrew. I had no idea why. Usually when that sort of
thing happened I backed away, allowing whoever it was to stay
in their shell. But the wine and heat combined with my surprise
at finding him so charming, and I persisted.

"Tell me why."

"I'm half Spanish. He speaks to that part of me, someone
my aunt once called the torero."

It was an interesting but not very forthright answer. I waited
as he poured what remained of the sauternes into our glasses. He
swirled his thoughtfully, and when he looked at me again I knew
I wanted to know him better. He had emerged from his shell
and his eyes were suddenly bright, an expression I later came to
understand always came on him in a moment of candor.

"And because the Fascists murdered him," he added. "That
more than the other."

I knew about it of course. Lorca's fame had spread with his
death. I also knew there was more to it than that. He seemed to
be wondering whether I was simply making conversation, or
truly wanted to understand his connection to the poet. That was
when I realized he'd known him personally.

"You were friends," I said abruptly, afraid it sounded more
like an accusation than a discovery, but he didn't take offense.

"We were, though I only spent a few hours with him. It's a
long story."

"I'm patient."

He told me everything, speaking rapidly until he came to Guernica. Then he talked in broken phrases, forcing himself to go on. I don't know what came over me, but I reached out and put my fingers to his lips.

"Don't. You don't have to."

He took my hand.

"No. This is all part of the same thing."

He said that when he returned from Spain he had not written anything for months because he wanted to confront what happened there, but it was still too close. As his leg healed he realized that the year away from Paris had allowed him to see what he needed to do in *Afternoon*. It was almost finished.

"I can't say I like it, but it would be stupid to abandon it now. I feel I'm writing against the grain of reality. The Quartet was one thing before I went to Spain. It's something else now. I see Heinz as a parasite living off society. He isn't connected with anything. I no longer believe in my theory. I'm not sure what I believe in, except an obligation to Lorca. Some day he'll come back into my life."

He smiled then, and I could tell he felt better.

"Listen," he said. "How would you like to come to a funeral?"

"What?"

"I'm going to bury Heinz when *Afternoon* is finished. It just came to me. I've invested six years in him and there has to be a proper funeral. I want you and Claude and Monika, everyone at the club. What do you say?"

"That I'm happy for you."

I sounded more serious than I intended, certainly more serious than the fantasy warranted, but the fact of the matter was that I understood what lay behind his humor. He looked at me as if I'd struck a nerve, penetrated his consciousness. It was very intimate and he seemed to know that he should let it go. That it could happen but it couldn't be explored just then.

"It has to be done right, with a eulogy. What about 'I come

to bury Heinz, not to praise him?' St. Omer, you know St. Omer? It doesn't matter. He will be the keeper of the gardener's trowel I'll use to dig the grave. It will have to be large enough for three books and a matchbox for Heinz's soul. Afterward we can hold a wake at La Masia and get appropriately drunk."

I don't know what set it off, but quite suddenly I wished I could add something of myself to Heinz's grave. I imagined it large enough to hold my Men in the Clock. I laid them one on top of the other like cordwood, covered them with dirt, but they burst through. Joaquín's imagination might be strong enough to finish Heinz. Mine was no match for my visitors.

"Now, Ursula, what about you? We're both Berliners. Why did you leave? Who were you back there?"

I looked away, though I'm afraid not in time to conceal the pain in my eyes. Monika was a white dot in the distance, too far away to help. I remembered Joaquín coming into the apartment, my surprised exclamation. Those guttural words, spoken so quickly and without forethought, released memory. Since Joaquín had come through the door the Men in the Clock had been moving in the back of my mind. He had not closed it in time, and they had shouldered their way in behind him. Until then I had avoided their glances, forced them to stay in the shadows by using my conversation with him to distract myself, covering their faces with language. His question gave them new strength. Some were there on the blanket, some floated above the trees. Some were full-face, as in portraits. Others appeared in cameo-like profile. I knew that I could remember their voices. Joaquín had asked why I left Berlin and for a fraction of a second I thought I might not be able to lie. For that tiny fragment of time the Bois did not exist, Paris did not exist. Nothing was real except my companions. No one knew about them, not Monika, or Claude, or any of my friends. It was only because I knew that my life would fall in upon itself that I found the strength to resist, strength no different from that which comes upon a swimmer caught in a riptide, a climber who must pull herself up out of harm's way.

"Oh," I finally stammered, "there were many reasons. You know what it was like there."

I told the truth about my family, where we lived, Jürgen, Hans, but I covered the time afterward with the vaguest generalizations, concluding that the war and its aftermath had been hard on everyone and that it was too painful for me to discuss. And as I lied the Men in the Clock smiled, leered, enjoyed themselves. "You are not this woman," they said. "He is very bright," they said. "You must be careful, Ursula, because he may discover that you lie. He knows how to listen. What right do you have to be here?" But I fought them, fought their voices, their accusations and innuendos and won because there had been nothing else I could have done, because I felt humiliated but not sullied, not in my heart of hearts. I had justified my past years ago, even as I lived it.

I was speaking quickly, lightly, the relief of having gotten through my lies so strong that my voice rose a little, regained a softer timbre, seemed to come from my lips now, rather than my throat. I could hear the difference, and wondered if he could too.

He did. Much later it did not surprise me when he and I discussed that day to learn that he had been trying to decipher me from the moment we met. He said that as we talked under the tree the shape of my life seemed distorted, as if I had seen something terrible. "Your expression said that you had to suppress whatever caused that strange cast in your eyes because it was on the verge of harming you. It wasn't illness, I was certain of that. It had to do with loneliness, or fear. You were full of things I couldn't fathom, and I was determined to find the cause. You touched me, but I needed to know why you had to live with something that could put a gun in your hands."

That was our beginning. When I think of what I wrote yesterday I realize there seemed to be a direction pointing toward an increased closeness in our lives. We did meet, talk, make a certain contact, but I could go no further. I couldn't be fully with him because of the Men in the Clock. They were imprinted on my mind. I refused to name them—gave them numbers—but I couldn't be with Joaquín because One, or Two, or Three, sometimes alone, sometimes together with Four and Five and Six always demanded audience, pierced walls, floated in the air. Had I seen him more frequently we would have been a multitude, and I could not risk that confrontation.

We met occasionally over the next few months, but I never believed we would progress much beyond where we found ourselves that afternoon in the Bois de Boulogne. I suppose it would have gone on like that if he had not come to me the day the Nazis entered Paris.

Joaquín always thought of Paris in terms of the old arcades, especially the Passage des Panoramas. To him, Paris existed in the shelter of that marvelous structure, as if sheets of glass had been erected on the city's ancient walls to protect it from the elements and shield it from time's decay. It was a domed city that he wrote about, a place as free of foreign bodies as the air a bell jar traps.

For ten years he walked in the invisible shadow of those glass forms, basking in the perfect light they reflected. Then the clamor from the outside world, which he dismissed at first as nothing more important than the distant shouts of troglodytes in his Fatherland, shattered his preserve as the fabled tenor's voice breaks crystal. The day the Nazis attacked across the Low Countries horrendous noise poured through the fractured dome, even though the army was hundreds of miles away. Shards of glass fell from enormous heights, twisting in the air where they reflected a distorted sun before crashing into streets and sidewalks, tearing awnings from cafés and filling the métro entrances with sparkling rubble.

Signs were fixed to lampposts advising anyone not required to stay to leave Paris as soon as possible. Already people were fleeing in cars, and the train stations were crowded with refugees. After the attack on the Somme, the Ministry of Public Works brought construction workers in from the provinces to build defenses, and Joaquín watched them seal off streets he once counted as his own. Within days elements of the French army turned up—small groups of dazed, haggard men with defeat legible in their eyes and the way they walked—an army of transients without leaders or provisions, whose frightened, surly faces increased the panic of Parisians and sent them fleeing south in greater numbers.

Paris was declared an open city then in an attempt to save it from destruction, a place offered up to the Germans' delectation the way pimps send whores to clients in Pigalle.

The city and the county forgot their boundaries. Farmers from surrounding villages drove livestock through the streets, hoping to find refuge for them ahead of the advancing army. Shopkeepers pulled down metal doors whose ratcheting had comforted Joaquín in the early morning hours. Cafés filled with frightened, suspicious people. Workers walked away from the métro so that when he went down the entrance at the Opéra he was greeted by empty tracks and dark passages musty as the catacombs.

On the streets buses, taxis, private cars, trucks, sprinkler wagons, everything with wheels migrated to the south. Corners became midden heaps where garbage spilled over sidewalks. Burst suitcases lay abandoned in intersections, their contents spilled like entrails. Broken furniture, scarred bedsteads, and gleaming antiques became firewood for the taking. In every arrondissement people crowded the streets on bicycles, precariously navigating through lines of men and women pushing handcarts and baby carriages piled high with whatever household goods they were strong enough to salvage. Men, women, children and invalids flowed south in disarray, making for the highway that led to safety. They pushed, shouted, cried and ran in the purity of particular fear, but there was always time to look over their shoulders at the palls of smoke rising in the distance from burning oil depots.

Late in the afternoon of June 14 there was a knock at my door. I was tutoring one of my students, a little girl named Jeanne-Marie. As soon as I opened the door and saw him spattered with blood I turned and told her we were finished, quickly sending her on her way. As she passed him her eyes grew wide with fear and she ran off down the hall.

"I'm sorry," he said quickly. "Something terrible happened."

I stared at him with a mixture of shock and concern before I asked if he was hurt.

"No, but I could use a drink."

"But . . ." I stammered.

"I'll tell you later."

"You're sure nothing's wrong?"

"Everything's wrong," he said, "but it isn't my blood."

"Sit down," I told him. "The drink can wait."

I went to the kitchen for a towel, wet it, and when I came back in told him to stand still so I could clean him up.

It was a strange moment. I had no idea what had happened. I was stunned, surprised, aware that his unexpected appearance carried a certain intimacy and that it was blossoming even as we stood there silently and I washed his face. As I daubed at his forehead and the area beneath his scar I glanced at him. His eyes met mine long enough for a kind of recognition to pass between us, and as simply as that the barriers that held us apart collapsed. Five minutes earlier I had been helping Jeanne-Marie with her wretched English. Joaquín had not existed. Now we faced each other, closer than we had ever been, and as that knowledge passed between us I wanted to cancel it, but it was too late. I remember giving in with a sigh as I stepped back and surveyed my work.

"Now I'll get you a drink."

We went into the living room and then he told me everything.

He had left his apartment early in the morning and the emptiness of the city was apparent even before the sun reached the rooftops. The few people he encountered only made the streets seem more silent. The crescendos of sound that always accompanied the city's waking had been like ballast to him, and now, lacking weight, he seemed to rise over the streets and wandered more aimlessly than usual until noon, when he felt light-headed and was obliged to rest when he reached the Quai d'Orsay. From a bench shaded by a plane tree he looked down the avenue, which ran on and on, like an exercise in perspective ordered by inconsequential trees rising absurdly from metal grilles set into the sidewalks. A stray dog with gray fur and ragged ears came out of nowhere, ran twice around the bench and sat down a few feet away, ears back, eyes focused, clearly wary of Joaquín. When he called to the dog it would not move. An old couple hurried by on the far side of the avenue. The woman pointed at him, the man nodded, and they turned up a narrow alley, the woman looking over her shoulder as if to make certain that he would not rise and follow them.

It was very quiet. The dog scratched its neck with an ungainly back foot. A few birds sang. It was a particular silence, not that of the countryside, or the dawn, or the early morning hours. This was the silence of a vacuum of the stillness said to lie at the center of a storm. He thought of the colors that were supposed to be visible in that center, imagined a certain shade of yellow slightly paler than Pernod left in the bottom of a glass.

Almost imperceptibly, the vacuum filled with sound. At first, he could not even tell what direction it came from, so faintly did it disturb the surrounding air. Only gradually did he realize that it was out there in the distance on the avenue, a sound that could have come from below the pavement, or from the air, but which finally resolved itself into the black shape of a motorcycle and sidecar.

He watched it approach with no particular interest because he could not conceive of the riders having any possible relationship to him. The sound became louder, more aggressive, and soon he saw the German soldiers, their uniforms the color of the pigeons who frequent the Boulevard St. Germain. The driver had slowed down, and because he saw their faces so clearly, the sense of apprehension that had come upon him slid away. Neither the driver nor his companion was more than twenty. Their cheeks were red and hearty as country boys', and he found it oddly amusing that they wore those Prussian steel helmets, rather than comfortable cloth caps.

It was an interesting moment for him, the kind of thing writers attend to. He was such a creature of habit that he instinctively reached for the notebook in his breast pocket, already having a notion of how he might describe those peasant faces so incongruously wreathed with steel. As his fingers closed on the notebook the motorcycle turned out of the middle of the street, approaching him faster and faster. There was a blending of speed and sound, the almost leisurely putt-putt of the motor becoming steadily stronger, a high-pitched whining sound compressed by the snoutlike exhaust pipes trailing by the back wheel.

Then he saw that the man in the sidecar was holding a pistol. It looked huge and black in the midday sun, but the soldier cradled it almost casually, half pointed at the sky. A moment later it was leveled at Joaquín. It happened so fast that there was not even time to be afraid, or for his mind either to register the bizarre nature of the event or to find its meaning. The gun barrel grew as large as a cannon's mouth as the motorcycle picked up speed until it seemed that he might rise and touch the pistol that was about to end his life.

He understood his mistake only when the yellow light flashed and the bullet tore into the dog. A spume of fine misty blood erupted from the dog's body like a fountain, and as the blood spotted Joaquín's clothes, wet his face and hands, the body skidded across the sidewalk, trailing a long red intestine before finally coming to a stop at the base of a lamppost where it sagged into a motionless heap of bloody fur.

For a moment he was confused because there was something else besides the dead dog, the hum of the engine growing less distinct. He did not know if it was merely fright that made him feel this other thing, merely rage and contempt for the Nazis, or something his mind would not release because it was unthinkable. Only after he pivoted on his left foot, only when his right foot came down and he felt the hard surface of the sidewalk did it come to him. The empty boulevard, which he had enjoyed during years of wandering, was now a set of bars. That loss became real to him in an instant, and as he hurried away, repulsed and frightened, its impact entered his consciousness like a scalpel.

Until that moment he was like everyone else confronted with great events in history, which are almost always seen out of the corner of the eye in an oblique, fleeting glimpse. For those not present at the scene the powerful, devastating, or perhaps merely symbolic event is even more fragmentary and at the mercy of the photographer's eye, the reporter's words, pictures and stories both imposing frames and suggesting the artifice of a beginning, a middle, and an end.

But sometimes the power of such a moment, its meaning and consequences, are captured with the clarity of a dream. As he watched the motorcycle growing smaller in the distance, the day entered his memory in the sharp image of the disemboweled mongrel skidding across the sidewalk. It did not remain a mere heap of fur and blood and bones. He said the creature sat in his mind like a queen at the opera, calmly surveying the destruction of her freedom. Combed, curried, diademed and serene, the dog sat in a richly upholstered box staring at the emptiness of Paris, panting, tongue lolling from a corner of its mouth as blood stained the velvet railing. Calmly, impassively, it stared.

It never occurred to him to return to his apartment, change his bloody clothes, wash the fine spatter of blood off his face and neck and hands before he came to me. As he walked he felt the pointillist dots coagulating, drawing his skin tight, the way a painter stretches canvas. People shied away as if he were a leper. He wanted to explain, take them by the arm and tell them about the dog, knowing that even as he spoke they would be more repulsed and frightened. As he went along narrow streets and alleys he scattered people in his wake.

"When the Nazi pointed his gun it was like I was seeing my body waiting for the bullet, but I was elsewhere, above, below, I can't say, but my body was a separate thing that was going to be destroyed."

I felt my expression changing as I listened, felt a shudder, became aware of the old despair and hoped that he didn't know that his memory touched an older one in me, for as he described the scene I remembered how I watched myself going up the Seven Dolphins' stairs into the harsh light of the narrow room, feeling exactly as he did. But he did notice, and he was clearly convinced that he had offended me. Much later he said that was the only construction he could put upon my sudden remoteness. It was as if I had drawn my palms down my face, as Muslims do at prayer.

"I'm sorry," he said. "I have no right bedeviling you with this."

I told him I was glad he did. "You've had a shock," and I tried to cover my confusion by getting him another cognac.

After I poured it and sat down again I regained my composure. I was present again, not as intimately as before, but not distant.

He asked what I would do and I said I didn't know. I looked away as I answered, but not soon enough to hide my tears. I apologized and brushed them away, adding, "I don't know if I can stay."

He wanted to help, that was clear, but he did not understand.

"Perhaps it won't be so bad—" he began, then stopped short. "What is it, Ursula?"

"I detest uniforms," I answered. "I don't know if I can live with uniforms."

I glanced out the window in an effort to regain control, but it did no good. Already I heard the clock chiming.

He rose quickly, and as he knelt beside the chair he took my hand. I didn't know what to feel. I was both afraid to have crossed that barrier between us and glad that it had happened. I allowed my hand to lie limply in his, wishing that he had stayed on the sofa, glad that he was close. I ran my other hand across my eyes, humiliated that I could not stop the tears.

"I have no right to let you do this," I said, looking down at our hands. "We must forget it. It is not for me."

"What is?"

I looked at him for a long time before answering. Of course I couldn't tell him, but in those few seconds I wondered what would happen if I did. What he would look like, what he might say.

"I think only our friendship, the way it has been. Believe me, it's best that way."

I tried to smile, but I'm sure I botched it.

"I'm glad you came," I said. "I'm sorry for what happened."

"I should have gone home first."

"No, but perhaps you should now," I said, withdrawing my hand. Suddenly I was quite exhausted. The clock was chiming in my head, and now the one in the church down the street struck three times. I felt surrounded and could not tell him. He was too close. Everything, it seemed, was too close.

"What is it?" he asked. "The scent you wear?"

I suppose it was only natural that he would make that remark about my perfume. I knew he was trying to return us to that moment when we had stood so close together, and I knew that he realized his mistake.

"I'll go now."

"Yes, I think you should."

At the door he turned and suggested that we all have dinner soon.

"Yes," I said, "that would be pleasant, but you must forget this, Joaquín."

He had opened the door, but now he paused with his hand on the knob.

"Why?"

It was too much. Too many things had come together during the last hour. The Nazis, our sudden rapprochement, the clear intimation that my visitors were coming. He had no way to know what his question meant to me, what would be dredged up. I felt closer to him than ever. I wanted to keep the feeling and I wanted to be honest.

"Please. If I told you, you would despise me. Let things stay as they are. Sometime—" But I did not finish. I could not conceive of a sometime and it seemed dishonest, a cheap unspoken promise I could never fulfill. I felt tired, old, haggard, beyond language, and so I waved and turned away even before he left.

I was much affected by Joaquín's tender regard, by his question as he paused, hand on doorknob. My answer, abrupt, slightly imperious, was intended to distance and injure him. While I had deliberately tried to discourage him for his own good, I felt guilty when I recalled how he trembled as I daubed at the fine spume of the dog's blood—a slight frisson perceptible through the damp cloth. I tried to keep his face before me, the sound of his voice, the surprising sense of closeness. I wanted to hoard them, use them against the two young soldiers with fair hair and pale skin who had taken up residence in the room and made me feel shriveled and impotent. For the next two hours as I waited for Monika and Claude I sat in my chair watching them sprawled on the sofa, their legs thrust forward in polished boots. I knew they were the outriders of the Men in the Clock, but they could have come from the moon. Some strange apparatus, odd as the machines of Jules Verne, might as well have brought them there. All afternoon they stared, and their eyes did not lose their luster even in the lengthening shadows.

Only when Monika's key rattled in the door did they vanish. She knew something was wrong the moment she saw me and the blood-stained cloth. I told her what had happened, repeated the story when Claude returned a little later. As we talked I wanted to escape. If it had been up to me, we would have left Paris as soon as the news came of the Germans crossing the Low Countries. I would have gladly walked, laden with whatever goods I could carry, to the train station. I would willingly have made the trip twice, three times, a dozen. But much as I wanted to leave, I knew it was impossible. We were tied to Paris by Claude's job. Still, I did not know if I could stay, and because of that fear I did not permit myself to think about what it was going to be like, now the Nazis were here. The future remained a cipher. I could not see it otherwise. I forced myself to think only of the next few days, trying to see them as malleable, open to options. I could endure day to day. What lay further off must be kept vague and undefined.

I was very tired. For the first time since the three of us had moved into the apartment I wished for more privacy. Pleading a headache, I went to bed early, and that was when my visitors finally came.

Usually they remained on the revolving platform, but that night it was extruded from the face of the clock like a huge tongue and they slid down it as if it were a staircase, stepping off the end into my room. They were all in uniform. A glass wall surrounded my bed, and they approached it in groups of two or three, pressing their hands against the glass, then their faces, like children outside a patisserie, and their faces looked as gleeful as childrens'.

"Relent," one said. I searched the faces to find who spoke. He was at the far end, an officer who frequented the Seven Dolphins.

"You were right to send him away," another said. "Be loyal to us."

Then there was applause.

"Let us in, Ursula. For old times' sake."

The glass bulged inward from their insistent pressure and I seemed to rise then and push against it, straining against their strength. The glass did not so much break as dissolve and then the officer was standing next to me, reaching for me. I could not feel my arms, and when I tried to scream a dead dog tumbled from my lips.

I woke with a start and snapped on the light, fully expecting them to be there. I could not believe it had only been a dream. I rummaged quickly through the drawer of the bed table for a sedative. I hated taking it because it numbed my mind for a day afterward, but I had no choice that night, so I took it and lay back, waiting for its effect. In a few minutes they began disappearing, like flies leaving a piece of food on a plate.

5

As the wake of the exodus washed over us we wondered if we were stupid for staying, or simply more brave and optimistic than friends and neighbors who had fled. There were no easy answers, and that contributed to our confusion. Not long before, the rhythm of city life which Joaquín had captured so eloquently in his novels had seemed as inviolable as carved stone. We worked, paid rent, bought food and clothes, made plans. But in the course of a few short weeks we came to understand the fragility of the future and saw it for what it was—a dream that can vanish in an instant when you wake to the rumbling of army trucks on a normally quiet street, or a Nazi yelling at someone below your window. Almost overnight connoisseurs of the future became keepers of memory. The way we thought changed, the

○

way we spoke. "Remember?" "I remember," "Do you remember?" became harbingers of other changes in language that the Nazis forced upon us.

During that time Claude and Monika and I tried to adjust to a new life, and we were no more successful than could be expected. I had news of Joaquín from Claude, who saw him on Saturdays at La Masia. He called once to say that he'd recovered from the Quai d'Orsay and that he was grateful for our afternoon. I was pleased to hear his voice but I refused to see him because I knew my pleasure would be choked by the Men in the Clock. Even while we talked on the phone I felt the old guilt rising, my face warm with it, my heart beating with distress as I remembered the sudden sense of intimacy, the moment of trust as he stood before me. Then I wished he hadn't come at all, that he'd gone to someone else.

A month later I felt stronger and realized that I wouldn't fall apart if we met from time to time. It seemed possible to have him as a friend. Besides, I was lonely. Most of my students had stopped coming and I had too much time on my hands. Reading while Claude and Monika were gone wasn't enough, and that was why I agreed to see him.

We were eating lunch when he told me about St. Omer's proposition. I'd made omelets—you could still get eggs then—and after I served them he said something had happened I might find interesting. It had to do with what we'd talked about the first time we met, when he told me that he was convinced Lorca would come back into his life some day.

One Saturday St. Omer arrived early at La Masia and talked nonstop for an hour. He had been looking for some way to respond to the Occupation, and it happened that a wealthy friend was willing to finance a clandestine newspaper. The man had interests in one of the dailies which had been taken over by the Nazis and turned into a propaganda rag run by their own people and some collaborators. This was his way of restoring the truth. The benefactor did not want to be involved directly and put St. Omer in charge. Jacques had already recruited several members of the Lorca Club and wanted to start working on the first issue as soon as possible. "No restrictions, Wolf," he'd said. "You can do whatever you want." Joaquín volunteered without a second thought.

That afternoon, as St. Omer explained the logistics of printing and distribution, Joaquín was already casting about for subjects. His first idea was to write about how his cousin Albert exemplified the Nazi mind. He started the essay the next day, but its ideas were too obvious. "Stupid. What anyone could say." As he crumpled the pages and dropped them in the wastebasket a bowl filled with the olive pits he'd taken from Fuente Grande caught the light from the windows giving onto the Rue Littré. He remembered María's question about Heinz and the torero. Until that moment the olive pits weren't anything more than mementos, but even as he looked at the bowl they had begun to germinate. He understood that he could use Lorca's story to illuminate what was happening in France. Suddenly, the broken glass of Paris rose into the air, like images in a film played backward. His memory of Fuente Grande and the war had made it whole again.

I have thought about that moment more than once. I go over it slowly, with a scholar's deliberation, intent upon the truth as I try to see it from various angles, rearranging things, emphasizing one in favor of another, but my conclusion is always the same, always shaped by a paradox. The inescapable fact is that the Nazis provided the means for Joaquín to redeem the past. Choosing to stay an extra day in Guernica had scarred him more severely than the Guardia's club. He never said so directly, but he didn't have to. I knew he longed to refashion himself in his own eyes. Yes, he had fought and risked his life for what he believed. No one would blame him for wanting another day or two away from the fighting. But he did, and because of that the Nazis *had* to come. I have often wondered what route he might have taken if they had bypassed France, and I am certain that he would have lived a life centered on an absence, embittered by having lingered in Guernica. The truth is that the town lay like a wound in his mind. He grieved for Ansaldo and his family, for everyone killed in the bombing, but he grieved equally over what he perceived as his own cowardice. That, finally, was why he stayed too long in Paris. He had to remain until he knew he was not afraid.

And so Joaquín reentered the arena he believed he had abandoned in Guernica, armed this time not with a rifle but a bandolier of words.

In normal times words can't match the velocity of bullets. In normal times they are not even the shadow of an act, merely its rehearsal, or its memory. But the Occupation changed the nature of words. Almost overnight the use of words, except by the official press, became an act of sabotage, no different from blowing up railroad tracks, cutting telephone wires, assassinations. People writing for clandestine papers such as the one formed by members of the Lorca Club and called *Les Ecrivains de la Résistance* discovered that their words had become corporeal objects, dense as stones, sharp as glass, and that inscribing them with pens on paper, typing them on ancient typewriters, printing them on mimeograph machines or presses was considered by the Nazis as no less dangerous than setting off dynamite, felling trees across country roads, thrusting a knife into the back of an unsuspecting officer as he entered a darkened métro stop.

That was why they sanitized the papers, why there were prices on the heads of writers. But they couldn't stop the voices. They remade the surface of Paris into a fortress but another city lived underground, an invisible city full of invisible people whose voices persisted in rising to the surface as if they were born in the catacombs beneath the Musée de Cluny, or in the sewers, or as if they had floated up through mysterious fissures in the ground and around the edges of manhole covers. The Nazis listened frantically for scratching pens, the tat-tat-tat of typewriters, the clanking of printing presses—actions as dangerous to them as crazed miners digging beneath their headquarters in the Hotel Crillon. At the Crillon, at Gestapo headquarters on the Rue des Saussaies, men in uniforms and men in leather coats and green felt hats angrily read these denunciations, these reports of the progress of the war and acts of sabotage. If they had a literary bent they might even have uttered appreciative comments about the quality of the writing as addresses were discovered, identities ferreted out, dossiers developed, pen names collated and codified. They posted men from the counterintelligence, the Abwehr, the Gestapo, and French collaborators on street corners, in shops and bistros, and eventually the web of which each man was a single sticky filament spread across the whole city. We knew they were trained in subtleties, that they were released into the city with the capacity to spot suspicious people, to detect actions, gestures, expressions, things that were wrong, or too right. They looked for everything—weapons, false papers, messages. At roadblocks and checkpoints they looked for confusion, listened for flaws in stories about where we were going, why we were there at that time of day. And they looked for specific faces too. Photographs were pasted inside the sweatbands of their hats, and many of us had stories to tell of seeing one of these men carefully remove his hat and check the faces there against those passing on the street.

If I were to draw this network on my map, I would show its concentric circles reaching from the defamed Hotel Crillon into the farthest suburbs. I would try to show how arrests, opportunities for surveillance, reports of suspicious persons and suspicious acts all traveled along the threads of that huge web to the center. Morning, noon, and night men who had been sent out to discover the sources of the underground voices returned to the center, unburdening themselves of information while four blood-red swastika banners snapped in the wind above the grand hotel.

Joaquín's voice must have offended them from the beginning. Many of the stories in *LER* straightforwardly reported on Allied victories and acts of sabotage gleaned from French-lan-

guage broadcasts on the BBC as well as information passed on
by members of the underground. But there were also speculative
essays, philosophical essays, and Joaquín chose that mode for
himself. From time to time St. Omer, Sandoz, and Feinstein all
wrote such pieces for *LER*. Others did the same for *Combat*
and *L'Humanité* and *Les Lettres Françaises*. Joaquín's essays
were oddities distinguished by parallels he drew between the
Spanish war and the Occupation. Fuente Grande became the
seedbed of his outrage, and its fruits had to be bitter to the men
charged with silencing the voices. Even now I can see them
impatiently thumbing through copies of LER they'd confiscated, looking for his column, *Letters to Lorca*. Part autobiogra-
phy, part history, part eulogy, they were always addressed to his
friend. The writers of the Resistance were impassioned people,
lyrical and precise in their denunciations. The *Letters* were all
that and more, for what he said was couched in a view of time
and place that broke the bonds of the verisimilitude he'd served
so faithfully until he'd gone to Spain. I have them with me, a
thick packet wrapped in a sheet of oilcloth purchased the day
before I left Lisbon. Claude believes we may find a publisher in
America, and while that would greatly please me, it is less important than the comfort they afford because they invoke the real
Joaquín, and it is only fitting that he be allowed to speak for
himself from time to time as I try to conjure up his life here on
this windy deck.

The first letter showed the stony world of Fuente Grande.
He took us in among the olive groves, along the teardrop shape
of Ainadamar, revealed the rooms of La Colonia, determined
that we should know these places with the clarity of photographs
or dreams:

Consider the last night of Lorca's life. After the *Gypsy Bal-
lads* he turned to darkness as if it were his true element, a
place crowded with knives and blood, love and vengeance so
that he was more prepared for the intimate shadows of La

Colonia than the others imprisoned with him there who would also be taken to the barranca of Víznar as soon as dawn slit the horizon. Since he was not a foolish man he was afraid, like the others, but his fear would have been tempered by the world of his poems where Spaniards like himself, Gypsies in heart, if not in blood, sought honorable deaths and clean memories. I believe his fear blossomed silently, that he held it inside himself, a single flower in a tulip vase, as he talked to the others with the same dignity that runs like a flame through his poems. Some were friends, especially the flamenco singer, Lorenzo, whose face was bruised and swollen from a beating by the chief Falangist of Granada, one Luis Valdés. Lorca and Lorenzo consoled each other and then fell silent when the village priest appeared to hear the believers' confessions. The sibilant Latin must have been heavy on the air even after the priest departed so that it was all the more remarkable when another voice sounded as Lorenzo began singing a cante hondo and soon everyone was clapping out its rhythm, voices and hands penetrating the ceiling to the rooms where the Falangists who would kill them slept. Some would have been awakened, and perhaps the defiant sound of that song might also have awakened them to the knowledge that they were there to kill men and women whose roots reached deep into the same ground. Others would have dreamed of the music. Either way, it had no effect on Valdés's men. At dawn Lorca and the others walked between the men who had listened or slept, walked to the barranca where the reports of the rifles scattered birds resting in the olive trees, the shots dying in the quick fluttering of wings.

Fuente Grande is silent now. One hears only the trickling waters of the acequia, wind in the olives and pines. But it is not empty. In that place at the end of Archbishop's Road Lorca, Lorenzo, all the others must have a kind of life. They do in my imagination, and in that of people I have met. I see them gathered at night around a fire of olive wood. Valdés is there too, condemned to look on and listen. In poor houses along the way, in farm houses and shacks scattered across the vega, people are said to dream nightly of voices on the wind. Gamblers in cantinas pause in their talk, and as they set aside their cards they hear more than the plash of water from the acequia. People in the village, peasants in the country assert that on certain nights the glow of a distant fire lights the sky above the barranca of Víznar.

St. Omer had assured him that he was free to say whatever he liked, but a few days after *LER* appeared for the first time he took Joaquín aside after the meeting of the Lorca Club had ended. He had had dinner with their benefactor the previous evening, and while the man was pleased with the issue, he did not understand the letter. "He asked what good this material about Lorca would do," St. Omer said. Then he looked at Joaquín skeptically. "I have to say he has a point. In any case, he wants to see you."

They met in an apartment on the Right Bank where an old man let Joaquín into a darkened room. The only light was from a fire and he'd been startled when the benefactor spoke from the shadows on the far side. "I prefer that you not come closer. It's best that you not see my face. I am not so brave as you and the others, that is the first thing I want you to know. The second is that I admire your work. The problem is that I am not clear about what you are doing, or why."

Joaquín explained that in shedding light on what happened in Spain he had found a way to place the Occupation in a broader context.

"But it is France that concerns me."

"And me," Joaquín answered. "Lorca's fate is ours. I can do something with it, but if it isn't to your liking, I'll resign."

The benefactor moved to the fire and was outlined against the light.

"An ultimatum?"

"That's your word, not mine. This is the way I can contribute. There's more to come, and when you see it, perhaps you'll change your mind."

The benefactor prodded the fire and then took a few steps forward, coming close enough so that Joaquín saw a shock of gray hair and the glint of several rings.

"I was only worried about your commitment. So long as you feel this strongly, I think you should continue. I am a patient man. May I ask a final question? Why do you see what is happening here through Spain?"

"I was there," he said. He knew immediately that that simple statement was not enough. Now that the man had accepted what he wanted to do he owed him a fuller explanation.

"I was there," he repeated, "and this is no different. The same things have happened and the same things are going to happen. It will help to show that."

"St. Omer told me that you were wounded in Guernica."

"Did he say why? What it cost?"

"No."

"A man is only as good as his acts."

"Guilt?"

"A way to repay a debt. We do what we can at the time."

"So long as it sheds light."

"Trust me."

The man turned away then, and as he did Joaquín caught a glimpse of his bony face before he retreated into the darkness.

"Go and write about your friend."

He told me about the meeting the next day, while we were walking. We'd reached the Place de la Concorde by then, and what I saw distracted me from his story. I had not gone out much for several weeks. On the Rue de Seine we did not see many Nazis. That was no surprise since it's a sleepy street of apartment buildings and not a thoroughfare. Now it seemed as if the whole German army had descended on Paris. The avenue was jammed with large, noisy trucks of transport companies bearing insignia of firms in Dresden, Munich, Stuttgart, Hamburg, Berlin.

"They're looting. Look."

He pointed to a blue truck backing up to an elegant home at the corner of the Rue St. Florentin. Four men in dull gray overalls climbed out and entered without knocking. A distraught woman stood by the door as they carried out furniture, silver, paintings. I'd never seen anyone so frightened and insisted that we go on because I couldn't bear to watch.

In a while we saw the red banners above the Hotel Crillon. In the distance the white dome of Sacré Coeur rose above Montmartre. The marble sculptures of the Concorde, the huge women meant to represent the cities of France, seemed like travesties of the order they were supposed to symbolize. Joaquín and I were the only Parisians in the Place. No old man, no young mother pushing a stroller, no private car, nothing but trucks like the one backed up to that house. Makeshift road signs were everywhere, replete with arrows and directions in German. Military cars went by at amazing speed. I told him that I had had enough. I felt vulnerable in my apartment, but this was worse. There was a sense of jeopardy, helplessness.

"What is it?"

I told him and he said that we should take time to go to the Arc de Triomphe. "There's something there that will make you feel better."

It almost worked. The monument had become a tourist attraction for Nazis disgorged from vans. They lined up, marched beside a lecturer who read a list of Napoleon's conquests, told them how the twelve avenues converging on the monument were named for military heroes. I knew why Joaquín had insisted on our going there. The Nazis were frightfully bored. They appeared harmless as cows, stupid, dull, plodding. But they were ready to obey. That was all I could think about. They would do whatever they were told. Things seemed worse to me on the way

home, and the feeling was compounded when I realized that the
hundreds of Nazis I'd seen had encouraged my visitors. I left
Joaquín abruptly at the door and quickly drew the blinds. No
faces hovered in the room, but I could hear them whispering. I
remembered the woman standing beside the entrance to her
house, tears streaming down her face. Sorry as I was for her, she,
at least, presided over a finality, and I was tempted to raise the
blinds and fling open the windows, to shout, invite them to
come in once and for all and take whatever remained of me they
wanted. I could think of nothing better than watching them
going down the Rue de Seine, some crouched on the top of the
van, others in the back, looking out. Emptiness floated out before me, as sweet and desirable as love.

By the time the second issue of *LER* appeared Rodríguez
had cleared out a storage room in the back of La Masia for them
to use as an editorial office, one of several places St. Omer summoned Joaquín to when it was time to assign stories or discuss
strategy. The room had two advantages. Since the Lorca Club
met every Saturday, there was an obvious reason for so many
people to gather there. They even went so far as to post a sign in
the window announcing the agenda for the following Saturday's
meeting. Normalcy and routine were the best covers for their
work, and they were all conspicuous about something that had
begun as a very private gathering of literati.

The second advantage of La Masia's back room was that
nobody who didn't know about it would have guessed that it
existed. Rodríguez had it built when he bought the café, and it
could only be reached by going behind the bar and through the
kitchen. There was no back entrance, only a thick brick wall.
When they needed to meet, someone was posted at one of the
sidewalk tables as a lookout. He sipped coffee or drank beer, and
gave a prearranged signal that meant no one was coming up the
street who might think it odd that so many patrons were slip-
ping behind the bar and disappearing into the back. Since the
café was closed to everyone but members of the club on Satur-

day, it was as safe an arrangement as they could desire. In any case, they felt more secure meeting there than at each other's houses or apartments.

Joaquín, St. Omer, Sandoz and Feinstein made up the editorial board. No one else was permitted in the back room, but sometimes Joaquín told me about what went on, and among his papers I found a handwritten list of events they discussed at a certain meeting that led to the first of several crises.

Sandoz, a one-eyed Czechoslovakian Gypsy, had been writing about partisans killed in street battles while trying to escape arrest. He also wrote about acts of sabotage. On the day in question Sandoz told them he wanted to do a summary piece, something that would shock their readers. He thought it might appear regularly as a kind of running commentary on Nazi outrages. Joaquín took out a fresh sheet of paper and they began listing the events they thought might be included. The list is incomplete, and all the more chilling because I have no way of knowing how many other incidents of the kind occurred. It is divided into monthly sections, and I reproduce it here just as it is.

JULY: A baker executed for taking part in a forbidden celebration of Bastille Day. Another man, a waiter, perhaps named Leconte, shot for having sung the "Marseillaise" at the same meeting.

AUGUST: Near Porte d'Orléans a Nazi officer stabbed to death. Six days later two mechanics from Porte St. Denis executed in reprisal. A Nazi sergeant killed in subway station near Montmartre. Cause of death unknown. Three hostages executed in reprisal. Also Count D'Estrene d'Orves and two other men captured on a mission from de Gaulle's London headquarters. Guillotined.

SEPTEMBER: Nazi officer shot at midnight on the Pont du Carrousel. The collaborator Marcel Gitton executed by underground. Nazi private shot. Three hostages, all women, publicly executed. Three Nazi noncoms shot. Ten hostages killed in reprisal. Twelve more hostages executed. Guillotining of Jean Catelas.

OCTOBER: Nazi commander at Nantes killed in town square. Forty-eight hostages shot. Officer killed in Bordeaux. Four hostages executed.

NOVEMBER: Nazi bookstore near Sorbonne bombed. Nazi restaurants bombed. Nazi doctor strangled near Boulevard Magenta. Three Nazi officers killed, eight wounded in restaurant explosion. Twenty hostages executed in reprisal.

They passed the list around the table and finally agreed that Sandoz should focus on the execution of hostages. At about that time Feinstein came in, apologizing for being late. As he took off his coat a yellow star shone against his jacket. He tried to make a joke of it, saying that the Nazis had made him pay for it with a textile rationing card. "I have to wear it everywhere," he said, "but I put on my coat so no one would see my little beacon when I came in."

Feinstein was no longer invisible, and because of that his work as a courier had to end. He had belonged to the Lorca Club from the beginning on the strength of his reputation as a minor poet. When *LER* was founded he seemed perfect for the work of the go-between. At that time he still held his post at the Louvre as a writer of descriptive materials for Acquisitions. After he was fired because of his Jewish blood he went to work as a baker's assistant, rationalizing his demotion by saying that it gave him even better cover, but even he knew he could not continue.

Joaquín replaced Feinstein, arguing that he had more time than anyone else to travel the sometimes long distances that were required. The underground papers operated autonomously, but from time to time the people who ran them needed to exchange information. Soon after Joaquín took over for his friend a man appeared one Saturday at La Masia just before it closed for the meeting. He brought a message from Jacques Decour, the editor of *Les Lettres Françaises*. Decour had been a friend of Joaquín's and St. Omer's since their early days in Paris, and had worked on the first issue of *LER* before he broke with them over a question of strategy and founded his own paper. Neither *LER* nor *Les Lettres* was proprietary about what it knew. The courier from Decour said it had to do with certain changes in the Nazi high command, and Joaquín immediately arranged a meeting with his friend in a little square not far from the Gare du Nord. They would arrive there exactly at noon, each entering the square from a different direction. If everything appeared normal, they would proceed to a café a few blocks away which was run by a man with ties to the underground.

Joaquín spent the early part of the morning working on his next letter. For the first hour he wrote swiftly and was pleased with his progress. Then something happened. When he recalled it later he said that he thought it was only a change of mood that sometimes came upon him when he reached a point where he had to consider a shift in his narrative. But that was a familiar feeling, and this was different.

At that time he was still relatively new to the invisible world. Everyone who worked for the underground papers had to learn the rules of invisibility, and sometimes he felt like a schoolboy preparing for examinations as he went over the rules for survival.

Never write anything down that might incriminate you or your colleagues.

Never carry a gun.

Never let anyone know your address.

When you leave someone, always go off in the opposite direction you intend to take.

Never wait.

Never develop a pattern in your daily life.

But the most important rule was the most difficult to learn because it relied on intuition, rather than knowledge. Survival depended on a sixth sense, on learning to trust your feelings.

People who in normal times approached the world with a tough-minded regard for reality discovered premonitions and became adepts of the mysterious. Intuition had the power to cancel meetings, kept people inside for days, sent them into the streets at unexpected times. All rational thought, a whole segment of knowledge that had been pushing forward in time since the Enlightenment, fell away in the face of this necessity to return to a world of signs and portents where each man and woman dedicated to the invisible world read dreams and feelings with all the conviction of a fortune-teller.

Joaquín was not immediately taken by this strangeness, but he was cautious and when he glanced at his watch and saw that it was only ten-thirty he was relieved that he would not have to leave for another half hour. He returned to his letter and found the thread again when the sensation returned even more strongly. He said that he felt as if people he couldn't see were looking at him. The distraction was so intense that he couldn't go on with his writing. He tried to busy himself around the apartment but the feeling remained, a nagging sense of an unde-fined presence, like a dream one knows occurred but which can't be recalled in any detail.

By then it was eleven-fifteen. If he didn't leave within the next few minutes he would be late for the rendezvous and the meeting would have to be rescheduled. Decour would not stay beyond the appointed time. Since the deadline for taking mate-rial to the people who mimeographed *LER* was the following afternoon, he couldn't afford to miss Decour, so he quickly put on his coat and hurried down the stairs, telling himself as he went that he was being silly. He felt better on the way to the Montparnasse-Bienvenue métro stop, but when he reached the stairs leading down from the sidewalk he had to force himself to enter. It was as if a powerful wind had sprung up, trying to blow him back to the street.

The train came and he let everyone else get on first. He stepped on board, then retreated to the platform. People looked at him suspiciously. When the next train arrived he went in immediately, found a window seat, and did not look at any of the passengers. The tunnels passed in a blur. He counted the station signs as they emerged from the darkness, little white squares bearing flying words. He rode past his stop to the next, even though it meant he would have to hurry once he was on the street.

Everyone appeared normal when he emerged from the stop. It was five minutes to twelve. He gauged his stride as if he were regulating a clock. The precision of his approach to the square pleased him. Everything was where it should be. People on both sides of the street looked as they should. He saw the trees of the square in the distance, and they reassured him. Soon only a block separated him from the square. A sense of relief passed over him and he was on the verge of laughing at his groundless fear when he crossed an alley and noticed two Citroëns traction avant parked on the left side, just where the alley opened into another street. He slowed down, conscious of walking too fast. That was when he saw three men standing in a knot beneath the plane trees at the entrance to the square. Two others, obvious in their overcoats and hats, drank at a sidewalk table across the intersection. He thought one of them was watching him and he went on, walking almost leisurely as he skirted the square and ignored the temptation to glance in that direction in the hope of at least catching a glimpse of Decour. He walked all the way back to the river.

No one knew who betrayed Jacques Decour. It could have been bad luck. It was equally possible that an informer had given away the time and place of the meeting. They tightened security, altered procedures, looked over their shoulders even more than usual, but the real or imagined danger for Joaquín and St. Omer was less important than their grief. A week after Joaquín passed the square the Nazis announced Decour's execution. That he feared it would happen did not lessen the shock of seeing his friend's name on the handbills the Nazis had begun to put up on lampposts. That Saturday Decour's name was added to the list. Joaquín insisted on writing the story, and while I admired it, I also knew that he had crossed a line, exposing himself more fully than before. He was beginning to take greater risks in his letters, but the piece on Decour that appeared in the next issue of *LER* could only have been read as a challenge. It is one thing to insult your enemies in plain language, reviling them for their stupidity and bestiality. They might even tolerate being cursed, or taunted, dismissing it as the kind of thing children do in schoolyards. After all, such language is expected, and they become inured to it. But it is quite another thing to say such things in the richer language of metaphors and similes. Power abhors figures of speech because they have the capacity to shatter masks and poses. That was why the Guardia hunted Lorca down, and that was what put the Nazis on Joaquín's track as well. He called the Decour essay "A Hundred Statues," and this is how it goes:

> The Nazis love their stolen city. Pass the Eiffel Tower, the Arch of Triumph, the Chaillot Palace, the Louvre, the Tuileries, or the Luxembourg Gardens and you can see them consuming our culture in the same way they steal furniture and paintings, with a kind of mindless gluttony. But their deepest love is reserved for the statuary of Paris, those stone and bronze figures set high above them on blocks of granite.
>
> We can understand why the Gestapo killed Jacques Decour by entering their minds as they gaze appreciatively at these figures. They are strong-willed, these Gestapo, and nowhere is their strength more obvious than in their desire to render all of us immobile as statues. Only when we are motionless and they are free to walk around us savoring their power will they be satisfied. To them, the power of the Thousand Year Reich is like the clouds of volcanic dust that fell on Pompeii, arresting people in the various motions of

life, whether they were drinking from a silver goblet, painting a fresco, or making love.

The Gestapo killed my friend because he refused to become figured marble, or cold bronze. They killed him because he had the courage to move his head and watch as they tried to make the rest of us as still as the statues they admire. Decour's crime was that he wrote about what he saw, refuting their vision of us as helpless creatures frozen into silence like a hare pinioned by his own fear in an open field.

Decour makes the Gestapo dream in their offices on the Rue des Saussaies, in the houses and apartments they have confiscated. He comes back to life, rising from an unmarked grave as they drift off to sleep thinking of better ways to bronze us. And it must be maddening when, in their dreams, they find themselves admiring our stone shapes and then see something amazing. Perhaps this particular Gestapo officer I am thinking of was the one who pulled the trigger and watched Decour die. Now he studies the faces of the statues, and to his horror discovers that he is surrounded by stone faces whose features are identical to Decour's. Every detail is right, down to the mole on his left cheek, and the way his left eyelid drooped. Hundreds of Decours move their stone mouths in his dream. Some raise stone hands and point. Others shout with bronze mouths. Still others kneel and make of their pedestals stone desks where they write and write and write.

When this officer wakes in a sweat and snaps on the light beside his bed, a hundred Decours remain in his mind's eye. He gulps a glass of water, a schnapps, but the dream persists. He can hear the scratching of stone pens. Caught between sleep and waking, this Gestapo cannot control his world. Decour is like a magic character in some folk tale, say a knight whose severed head grows back no matter how many times a broadsword passes through his neck. The Gestapo knows that each of us who remains alive speaks for Jacques

Decour, that his voice and ours are indivisible. When this officer goes to work he will have shaken himself out of his dream of the speaking statues sufficiently to believe that he and his comrades can find all the Decours in Paris and the countryside. He cannot allow himself to think otherwise. But the truth lies beyond his conviction. In that part of his mind which knows that the Master Race is only a myth, he will always know that he can kill Jacques Decour, but that he is helpless in the face of the idea of Jacques Decour, whose voice is not in the man he shot but in the hundreds of us who are even now writing Decour's thoughts, as if taking dictation from the dead.

6

The sun was setting on the horizon yesterday as I copied Joaquín's words. The sea spread out like a pale fan and everything seemed suspended in the light. Lorca's Gypsy searched the hills hopefully as her smuggler returned from the sea, still invisible to the Guardia waiting in some arroyo. Joaquín went up the mountain path with steady, unfaltering steps.

I gave myself up to the illusion, wanted to hoard its sense of stasis. I was succeeding when Claude floated into view. The wind tossed his curly hair as he bent over, extending my scarf and gloves. "I thought you'd need these," he said, adding that we'd been invited to dinner with the captain. He looked down at me as if I were a child, and I told him to stop patronizing me.

I was angry that I'd lost the moment and decided then and

108

there to be more firm with him and Monika. I've told them about what I'm doing, that now I can think about what happened without going to pieces, but interruptions send everything awry.

Dinner was awkward and uncomfortable. During the day the captain goes about in an old frayed sweater, but last night he wore a fine jacket with gold buttons and a hat fretted with insignia. There were five other passengers besides ourselves, Emma and Kurt, Marguerite and Jean-Paul, an old Spaniard named Francisco. Everyone would have preferred dining alone in their cabins, as we've been doing. We talked about the weather, passed the battered serving dishes, pretended to enjoy ourselves without revealing the slightest thing about who we were. What should the captain expect from refugees who've salvaged stories too raw to be shared? To his credit he quickly saw that he'd made a mistake. A sudden compassion came into his eyes, and all through dinner he repeatedly assured us that we would reach America as soon as possible.

Afterward I went up on deck and walked for half an hour. I felt stronger than I had since leaving Lisbon, more convinced than ever that this work is fruitful and will bind our days together. Once a shooting star fell toward the east, reminding me of Joaquín falling in the snow. For a little while his death seemed as random as that arching light and the notion chastened me, closed off the pleasure I had taken in the bright black sky and the faint phosphorescence of our wake. But later, as I lay in bed trying to accommodate myself to the ship's rhythmic rise and fall, I knew that that tiny event in the sky was no model for his life or mine. Unclear as it is sometimes, the sense of a design in all that happened reasserted itself, as did the conviction that I must piece it together in these pages.

The essay on Jacques Decour came back and suddenly the pattern leapt ahead, demanding my attention. No doubt the essay caused the Nazis to redouble their efforts to identify Joaquín and uncover the *LER* operation. And just as it must have spurred them on, so it did Joaquín. By that time he had finished an exhaustive investigation into the circumstances leading to Lorca's arrest. The Falange had attempted to disguise his abduction with various lies, but he pieced together what happened with the same determination an archeologist brings to a site year after year as he retrieves this shard and that shard from the dust until, finally, he sees a vase, a plate, a wall. He read and collated stories from Spanish papers and several other countries until he amassed a thick file of clippings that gave him all the necessary details. Now Decour's betrayal sharpened his sense of what happened in Granada, and he began writing with a sense of urgency, aware that his own freedom was jeopardized, and all the more determined to complete his story of Fuente Grande.

Several weeks later the letter appeared in *LER*. I read it then, and again this morning, after having breakfast with Claude and Monika. The speaking statues of his Decour essay seemed to whisper of betrayal and defiance, offering parallels between Decour's fate and Lorca's. The words were dangerous, and I found myself thinking once again of the corrida and the strange rhythms that govern the ritual played over and over in Spain. I don't pretend to understand it. The public slaughter sickens me. It demeans both those who watch and those in sparkling suits of lights who do the killing. But it was a way for Joaquín to understand the history of his life, and I try to see it in that perspective. The charging bull and swirling cape, the cheering crowd and polished sword are less suggestive to me than the moments of calm that measure out the violence as precisely as meter does the lines of poetry. As I read the letter and thought of the interplay with what he so recently had said about the fate of Jacques Decour, I imagined the torero and the bull facing each other, eyeing each other, taking one another's measure. I saw the torero flick his cape, set himself for the charge. The death of one or the other seemed more real, more imminent at that moment of stasis than when the bull actually ran its heart into that gleaming blade, or the torero was lofted into the air, too stunned as he flew to feel the pain from the horn that had impaled him. With each letter Joaquín was reenacting that stasis, goading the Nazis to cross the carefully raked sand, exposing himself both to their horns and to the voice of someone in the crowd who might betray him. That is why I want the letter to be part of this work I fret over every day.

It was very hot the summer they killed García Lorca. Madrid had been sweltering in the July heat for days when he decided to return to Granada and stay with his parents at their villa known as the Huerta de San Vincente. Several friends warned him that the Falange in Granada were very full of themselves just then, but he ignored them. He thought only of that cool, lovely house and the scents of the garden's jasmine and nightshade which gave him the exquisite pleasure of lyrical headaches. Compared with the images and scenes of home, the Falange seemed no more dangerous than rowdy schoolboys. Besides, he was also looking forward to celebrating Saint Frederick's Day with his father, who was also named for the saint.

He arrived only to be greeted with the news that his brother-in-law had been arrested. The next day Franco's planes bombed the outlying districts of the city. But things quieted down after that and he began to feel truly at home once again at the Huerta.

One morning, as he sipped coffee, he saw two men studying the house through the garden's grilled gate. They left only to reappear at five o'clock with half a dozen companions. They pushed the gate open and quickly went up the walk to the front door where he heard one of them tell the maid that they wanted the caretaker's brother, whom they believed responsible for burning down a parish church. They searched the house top to bottom without finding the boy, and when they demanded the identities of everyone there,

111

Lorca came downstairs to intervene. He told them they had no right to enter his father's house.

"So it's you!" one of them said contemptuously, then unreeled a litany of abuse, reproaching Lorca for his politics, his irreligion, his private life. He was, the man said, nothing but a loathsome, dangerous parasite.

The Falangists were so frustrated at not finding the boy that they took his brother Gabriel outside, tied him to a tree, and whipped him until he slumped against the ropes. Afterward they entered the caretaker's building, pushed the boy's mother downstairs, and forced the rest of the family into the yard, where they threatened to shoot them. Lorca protested again only to be knocked down as Gabriel's mother begged the men to leave them all alone. She had recognized the leader and went up to him, holding her face in her hands. She told him that he must remember her, that she was the one who had wet-nursed him in their home village years ago. He was clearly embarrassed and shouted for her to shut up. "No whore's milk ever passed these lips."

As this was going on in the courtyard one of the maids, a girl named Angelina, led Lorca's nieces and nephews out the back door where they ran across the open fields to a neighbor's house. The man immediately called the Falangist headquarters. Apparently he had some influence, because soon another group arrived and stopped the beatings, untied Gabriel, and tended to his wounds.

But this was not the last time the men would come to the Huerta. During the earlier encounter, one of them had driven back to the Civil Government building and informed the leader, Louis Valdés, of Lorca's presence. He described Lorca's conduct in the matter of Gabriel's interrogation, and that was all the proof they needed to move against him. Lorca by that time had already attracted attention because of his work. Moreover, it was rumored that he was a Communist and operated a radio in the attic where he maintained contact with rebel leaders.

A friend of Lorca's, Angel Saldana, learned of the plan and called to warn him. Lorca immediately phoned the poet Luis Rosales, who arrived half an hour later in a car.

Lorca told him that he did not know who else to turn to, but he did not want to put his friend in danger. Luis did not listen. He said that Federico should leave Granada immediately. He could get him to the rebel zone. He had done it before with others. Lorca could not abide being trapped between the two sides, and he also rejected the suggestion that he could go to Manuel de Falla's house. They had recently quarreled about a poem of his that de Falla believed insulted God.

It was then that Luis decided to risk taking Federico home where he would be safe to think about his options. Luis gave very precise instructions to one of the servants, telling her to deny she knew anything about Lorca's whereabouts. If questioned she was to say that she had seen him running across the fields with nothing but the clothes on his back.

For the next eight days Federico lived in the sanctuary of the Rosaleses' house. Angulo Street was a sleepy place of three-storied, balconied buildings, a street so narrow that only at high noon did the sun disperse the shadows on the sidewalks. It should have been a safe place, but it was still in Granada, still in Spain, where safety anywhere was an illusion.

The Falange returned to the Huerta de San Vincente several times over the next few days. When they realized he had escaped, they abused his father. The leader, Ramon Ruiz Alonzo, pushed the old man against the wall and gripped his collar. "Tell me where that faggot of a son of yours is hiding. If you don't, I'll take you instead." García

Rodríguez looked contemptuously at Alonzo, who struck him in the face.

Conchita, Lorca's sister, could not stand it. Afterward she knew that she had made a terrible mistake, but at the time all she could think of was finding a way to stop Alonzo from beating her father. She gripped his arm. "He isn't hiding! He just went out to a friend's house to read poetry. They do it all the time. He hasn't done anything."

She thought it was safe to say that since there were so many poets in Granada, but Alonzo knew about Lorca's friends, and as soon as Conchita spoke he guessed that he had gone to Angulo Street.

During his stay at the Rosaleses' house Lorca kept his spirits up by talking about New York and Buenos Aires. Sometimes he played the piano. He was too disturbed to write, but he could read, and that was what he was doing when the Falangists arrived and took him away to the Civil Government.

In that hour the Falange believed that Lorca's life came to an end. The journey from sanctuary to darkness, sun to shadow, lay like a ritual prayer in the minds of Valdés and those who served him. Priests and true believers finger rosaries, and the Fascists of this world do the same, except that human beings replace the polished beads, and there is neither sequence nor hierarchy in their supplications. It is always the same. That day the bead of Lorca's life slipped between Valdés's thumb and forefinger. He pressed, and the soft pads of his fingers closed off the light just as the Gestapo's did when they led my friend Decour into their darkness.

But the Falange and the Gestapo made the same mistake. Time and again they each have felt life give way between their fingers. For some of those trapped in that way there is truly nothing more, and once they are crushed it is as if they never lived. That was the Gestapo's hope when they killed Decour, the Falange's when they prepared Lorca for

Fuente Grande. But in each case there was a miscalculation which they would not have been aware of at once. Valdés must have enjoyed several days, even a week of victory before he gradually came to understand that Lorca had another life beyond his reach. My friend Federico was killed because of his words, and those words had touched the minds of people with the colors of his beliefs and his emotions. Lorca entered the darkness conceived out of the same hatred and disdain that marks the limits of the Nazis' mind, but his words, even then, were alive in other minds. Sooner than Valdés was able to imagine, the sky above Granada grew heavy with Lorca's poems. Images of Lorca filled the eyes of old women walking close to plastered walls. Lorca smiled at Valdés from the glow of streetlamps, watched him from behind grilled windows overlooking silent squares.

Imagine Valdés's chagrin when he finally understood that in killing Lorca he gave new life to the poet's lyrical denunciations of Guardia and priests, chagrin shared by the Nazis who, in assassinating Jacques Decour, created statues speaking in the wind. Neither Falange nor Gestapo can touch their words. They would have to pull down the sky to stop Decour from dancing with Lorca.

Not long after the letter appeared—I think it was early the following week—Joaquín went to St. Omer's house for dinner and stayed the night. The next day he was walking home along the Rue de Rennes where he heard the music of a military band. Every day at noon in certain sectors of the city a squad of musicians appeared behind a drum major who set the beat with stylized thrusts of a glittering baton. He would be separated by a meter or two from the band, whose front ranks were given to the snaredrum players, followed by the horns and then a deployment of troops whose shoulders bristled with rifles. The music that they made insinuated itself into the mind with amazing ease since it was keyed to a kind of universal sympathy. Much as we hated the Nazis, Parisians gathered on the sidewalks when they heard the blaring trumpets, and it never failed to surprise Joaquín to see stern-eyed Frenchmen tapping out the rhythm as the band marched by.

To rid himself of the melody of "Deutschland über Alles" he hummed a song of Piaf's, then studied merchandise behind fly-specked windows in the hope that he could clear his mind. He was still distracted as he turned into the Rue Littré and saw two cars parked at an angle to the sidewalk, blocking traffic in both directions. His concierge, Madame Faverges, stood between two Gestapo officers. She was stout, and her flowered dress emphasized the thrust of her hips, her protruding stomach and pendulous breasts. She appeared to be arguing with the man in a long leather coat. Then the other, who was in uniform, began speaking rapidly, all the while thrusting a handful of papers under her nose. His head was tilted backward, as if he were looking at her through bifocal lenses. Joaquín could not tell whether she was more afraid of the papers or the officer brandishing them. At that point he had no idea what was happening. He thought she might have been caught hoarding, or in possession of forged papers, but then he understood that the men had come for him. He had been on the verge of continuing down the street, but he quickly returned to the Rue de Rennes and went on to the Boulevard Montparnasse where he walked all the way down to the Closeries des Lilas. He ordered a cognac, then another. The waiter asked if he wanted a menu but he shook his head, glanced at his watch, and stayed another hour before going back and entering the street from the opposite direction.

The Nazis had left. As he reached the foyer Madame Faverges's door opened a few inches, just enough to reveal one eye and a tuft of curly gray hair. There was a stifled sob as she emerged and quickly glanced outside. She was both angry and afraid as she told him that the Nazis had searched his rooms.

"I saw them outside," he said.

"They stayed a long time, monsieur. Half an hour at least. I convinced them you left yesterday."

That was all she needed to say. He knew she would not directly ask him to leave. Her lower lip trembled, and then she burst into tears. He told her not to worry and was about to go upstairs when she reached into the pocket of her housecoat and withdrew several envelopes. "These came yesterday."

He accepted the letters and then told her he was sorry. He would leave as soon as he could.

"Yes. Whatever you think."

The door of his apartment was wide open. He called for his cats, Rimbaud and Villon, but even as he spoke he knew they were gone. His books were scattered on the floor. The glass doors of the case where he kept first editions were broken. Every cabinet and drawer was open. The inkwell on his desk had been overturned and black India ink had soaked into the wood, leaving a dark stain. Sheets of paper and note cards littered the floor like yellow butterflies. The manuscript of his most recent letter was missing, but that did not bother him since he had a copy at *LER*. For some reason the Nazis had left his files intact, and for that oversight they would pay dearly because he would be able to continue.

In the bathroom the door of the cabinet above the basin hung on one hinge. The basin was filled with bottles, razors, bandages. He wet a towel and returned to the living room where he tried to clean up the ink, but no matter how hard he rubbed an egg-shaped stain remained. The marred surface of his desk was almost as painful to him as the loss of his pets. Both spoke eloquently to the fact that his life had been irrevocably altered. For the first time he was aware that he had lived every day of the Occupation with a false sense of security. There had always been the safety of his apartment, the certainty that he could return home and find refuge there. Now that zone had been violated. He could walk away. Part of him even then was arguing that he had done what he could and should immediately find some means to leave France. He never believed that he was made of heroic stuff. When he told me about the raid afterward he said that he was more acutely aware than ever before that he could not leave. He had a sense of duty to something outside himself that marked him more strongly than the visitation from the Nazis. The essential configuration of his life emerges in this moment I am trying to recreate. There was the sudden, self-protective response followed by his decision to stay. He was more distraught that his cats were gone than he was that the Nazis had traced him to the Rue Littré. He opened a window and called for them, aware that it was a foolish thing to do. It was more than likely that someone had been left to watch for him. He had already violated one of the cardinal tenets of survival in returning to his apartment, and that oversight became increasingly apparent in the next few minutes as he quickly stuffed a few clothes and his files into a bag.

Only when he was ready to leave did he remember his mail. One of the letters was from his publisher and contained a small check, enough for a month's rent. The other was from his father. Heinrich's handwriting had long ago lost its elegance, its smooth script giving way to the shaky penmanship of the very old. But as soon as he began reading he realized that the hand had also been encumbered by anger. It was, he thought, a day for betrayals. Somehow copies of the *Letters to Lorca* had reached Berlin. Heinrich called them "lubricious defenses of a pederast and libels on the Reich." He denounced Joaquín for his views, expressing shame and revulsion that his own son, his flesh and blood, was capable of treason. As far as he was concerned Joaquín had forfeited his place in the family. He was only glad that his mother had died before she saw what had become of him. In a young man, he said, such things might be forgiven. In a stupid, uneducated man, they might be condoned. But not in him. He told Joaquín that he was enclosing one final check from the trust, which had instructions to ignore any futher pleas.

While Joaquín read the letter I was at a friend's apartment

on the Rue Bonaparte. Before the Occupation I saw Madeleine Langlois infrequently, but during the winter we met once a week. Her husband had disappeared soon after the Nazis arrived. To everyone else she explained his absence by saying there was no work for him in Paris so he had gone to Rouen, where he found a job as a janitor. The truth was that Theo had joined the Resistance. She said no more, but by indirection, usually with some general observation such as, "Have you heard about the destruction of the tracks outside X?" she communicated what he was doing and always seemed extremely proud.

From time to time he returned to the city, and when this happened Madeleine would call and tell me she wasn't feeling well and hoped we could see each other the following week. But often the phones did not work and twice I went to her place, knocked, and heard quick footsteps. Then the door opened and she appeared in a dressing gown, saying she was sorry but she had a cold. It was our signal that Theo was there, and while I was always happy for her, I felt lonely going home.

But Theo was nowhere near Paris that particular afternoon as we drank ersatz coffee and tried to keep warm. As soon as I arrived she took me by the hand and led me to the worn green sofa. Things had calmed down only a while ago, she said.

"The Boches never bother with our street, but last night they were everywhere. I heard a commotion and when I looked out, it was still twilight, they were crawling over everything like a swarm of ants."

Her voice was shaky so I took her hand, trying to reassure her, but the wan smile I managed to coax from her quickly faded as she continued.

"They went to every apartment in the building. They beat on my door, and when I opened it three of them pushed by without so much as a word. They spoke German and I wished you were here so you could have told me what they said. They went into the bedroom, turned over the mattress, threw my clothes on the floor, demanded my papers, asked questions about

Theo, where he stayed in Rouen, that sort of thing. A little while after they left I heard them on the roof, and wished it was cold enough for ice so one of them, all of them, would slip. But they came back down and in a while they took the old man at the end of the hall, Pierre Callard. And I learned later that they found a radio and some Resistance pamphlets in Laval's place. It was incredibly stupid of him. I don't know why they believed me about Theo. There is no logic to it. It wasn't until this morning that I heard the rumor that they'd come because someone had killed a Gestapo not far from here. It might be true, it might not, you know how it goes."

Madeleine was strong and, everything considered, usually dealt with the Occupation better than most of us. I never heard her complain, but that afternoon she had used up her resources. Things were bad enough even if your life was above suspicion. With Theo off in the countryside blowing up railroad tracks and commiting all sorts of mischief the Nazis made her afraid for her safety as well as his. I stayed longer than I intended trying to console her.

By the time I left the Nazis seemed closer than they had in weeks. The watery light made Paris look old and alien, and when I thought of living under the Occupation for another winter I shivered and wondered how I was going to endure it. But I shrugged it off as best I could because there was no alternative, not then.

Claude and Monika were waiting with the news about Joaquín. He had gone to the university and told Claude everything. It was clear to me that he should leave France, but he had told Claude that was not something he could consider for a while. He intended to stay another month or two, however long it would take to finish his *Letters.* Then he would leave, though it was not clear where he might go. I was torn between wanting to give him refuge and concern over the changes this arrangement would make in all our lives. The apartment was not large, the three of us had had to make a number of concessions, but there was no choice. We would keep our rooms and offer him the sofa.

It was not until long after Claude and Monika had gone to bed that I allowed myself to think about what this would mean for me. I was drawn to Joaquín, but I had deliberately discouraged him from going further the day he told me what had happened on the Quai d'Orsay. Now I was going to be living with him, and the prospect both intrigued and frightened me.

•

Lorca's Gypsy and her smuggler seem very close. I have not forgotten them, not once, since coming up here a week ago to puzzle out my life, but they return now with a fine insistence. Surely, as their fate formed in his mind, there was a moment when he saw them drawing close and was surprised when all at once their lives twined around each other like vines circling the staffs of a trellis. As I think of the poem made to chart that tightening I feel all of us bound together, the Gypsy and her smuggler, Joaquín and me, Lorca and Joaquín. And this is no torturing of facts into a false symmetry.

I am thinking of the moment Lorca entered the building of the Civil Government. The way from Angulo Street to Valdés's headquarters led along Trinidad Street and the Plaza de Trinidad, about the same distance as from the Rue Littré to the Rue de Seine. Lorca was being taken to prison, Joaquín was headed toward a hiding place, though one not so grim as the poet's. But the pattern is there, and it extends to the consequences. Joaquín was caught in a vise, his freedom reduced from the limitlessness of Paris to a place barely large enough for him to breathe in. Lorca blossomed into legend, and Joaquín took that legend and made it known to the world that last winter of his life.

7

That winter was colder and more bleak than anyone could remember. We prayed for snow because then things were not so bad for a while. Snow transformed Paris into a picture postcard of mansard roofs and chimney pots. Its reflected light deepened the yellow patina of buildings along the avenues. The overall effect was so remarkable that one could almost entertain the illusion that things had changed, but the snow never remained for long. In no time at all the sidewalks and streets were covered with a filthy brown slush whose icy water seeped into the soles of shoes no matter how careful you were. Nothing was more effective than chilled feet in killing hopes and refocusing our attention on the unassailable reality of the Occupation.

Part of that reality was time, which had been distorted by

the Nazis. One of the most insulting things they did was to decree that henceforth Parisian time was German time. All public clocks were synchronized with Berlin's. Clocks in churches, post offices, cafés, bakeries, shoeshops, houses and apartments ticked to the Reich's chronometers. As a result, daylight came late in the morning, and when the sun finally rose, it shone on a city that seemed more German every day.

For weeks on end frost never melted from windows that did not face the sun. On especially cold days it remained everywhere, and if you were outside you might look up at hundreds of frost-rimmed eyes and be forgiven for thinking that Paris was no longer the City of Light but the City of Frost, a vicious parody of the benign world Joaquín had once imagined when everything seemed sheltered beneath a crystal dome.

We burrowed inside coats and blankets in the hope that if we went far enough we might find sufficient warmth. But we never did, not at home. Houses and apartments were frigid day and night. Hot water was a distant memory, and if we warmed a pan or two on the stove and tried to bathe, the delicious sensation of warmth was gone in minutes and we shivered as we frantically dried ourselves. Children cried at the threat of baths, and old people were convinced they were going to die.

Frozen at home, we went in droves to churches, as if we had become a city of true believers. Claude and Monika discovered those nearby that still provided heat and we went regularly, crowding in with neighbors around hot-air registers.

When the churches ran out of coal our devotions took us to the banks. Joaquín, disguised with a beard and severe eyeglasses lent him by St. Omer, led us there like a patriarch, and we all stood behind him, happy to wait while he withdrew a little cash from his rapidly diminishing account.

Soon everyone caught on and the clerks began checking people, making sure they had legitimate business to conduct. Before long we could not go to the banks; then it was the post offices, which were cold but at least better than our apartment. And there were always métro stations if we'd been out on an errand of some kind. They offered a buffer against the wind, and we stayed in them as long as we could countenance the stench.

Staying warm became an avocation. We envied Monika's job in the bakery because she could go into the back when there were no customers and stand beside the oven, gratefully doing anything the owner wanted in order to thaw out. At home, Claude prepared for his classes by putting on a wool turtleneck, two more sweaters, a heavy jacket and fingerless gloves. His students became woolen lumps trying to attend to what he said.

Food was our main priority. Everyone in the building became a scavenger. The generous ones shared tips, the selfish kept to themselves news of places where one might find something edible. Grocers on the Rue de Buci became lordly and rude. There were demonstrations, and arrests were made for hoarding.

The search for food began at five in the morning when the curfew was lifted. One had to be able to sleep very soundly not to be awakened by the clatter of wood-soled shoes on the sidewalks as neighbors went in search for that day's provisions. Joaquín was often with them. His confinement during the day stifled him, and he judged that going out for a while at dawn was safe. Not only could he get a breath of fresh air, but he could save the rest of us the time and discomfort of shopping. He pushed and shoved with housewives and pensioners for vegetables, butter, cooking fat. He plotted the exchange of ration cards like a chess player, picking through piles of wilted and sometimes spoiled turnips, rutabagas, and onions before he made his move. He went at the end of the week to meat shops, frequented black markets, sometimes biked long distances on the strength of a rumor, and always kept his eyes open for vegetables growing in plots.

Our household sprouted cages in the kitchen. We raised rabbits, and kept two chickens for their eggs. Some people in the building even had guinea pigs, and many windowsills held pigeon traps baited with a few crumbs of bread laid out beneath a bit of fishing net. When the rabbits were large enough to eat I dispatched them in the alley, with Monika's help.

While all of this was happening Joaquín and I followed a ritual of comportment that took us back to the day he'd come to me from the Quai d'Orsay and I'd drawn a curtain between us. My reasons were more complex than those of younger women who are confused about their feelings and want time to think about what further intimacy they might desire. My act came from pure necessity, and it is still difficult to believe that the curtain rose inch by inch, as if of its own accord.

From the day after he arrived and we were left alone for the first time we spoke very little. We were both deeply aware of the awkwardness, and to allay it Joaquín's gentle manner became exaggerated, as if the forms of politeness might, in themselves, ease our condition. His courtliness made me nervous. He walked quietly, and when he offered to perform household chores there was always a ring of formality in his voice that made me want to tell him to relax and live in the apartment as if it were his home, not a railway station or a restaurant. But such well-meant comments would have insulted him, and while he acquiesced to the distance I had initiated so long ago, we also progressed in that strange formality.

During the day the urgency to finish the *Letters* demanded all his attention, so that hours passed when he seemed only vaguely aware of my presence. I spent my time lost in books, but that became more difficult after Joaquín said that he would leave as soon as his work was done. He had no desire to endanger us. There was also a possibility that the children and I might do the same. Claude had made inquiries about a post abroad even before the Nazis came. After months of no response, he received an encouraging letter from a university in the state of California. I discounted it as soon as he told me, telling myself that any number of pitfalls lay in the way. It was too painful to think of freedom, and I forced myself to accept the frozen world of Paris as the only one I'd have.

o

There were long silences during which Joaquín stared at the page before him, or out the frost-shrouded windows as he tried to find the images for his *Letters*. Sometimes I knew what he was thinking, and when he asked me to read the day's work, I often found passages that corresponded precisely with what I had surmised. At first these recognitions seemed complete in themselves, innocent of anything other than the pleasure that comes when we discover our thoughts intersecting with someone else's. When I understood the true meaning of my intuitions I tried to step back, but it was too late. I had already strayed from my protective curtain, and was even then aware of feelings I could not ignore, despite the whispering of the Men in the Clock.

Perhaps it was because we both knew we had only a limited time together that we began talking more. In any case, I see those days like the final moments people have at railway stations when the only imperative is to speak in order to fill one another's memories as full as possible. We crossed the boundaries I had set because we were no different from other men and women. We too had experienced our moment of recognition, felt our field of vision narrow until we only saw each other. But we had not been free to take the next, necessary step into the story of one another's lives, which made us who we were, until one day when I put down my book to watch Joaquín at work. Quite suddenly I knew that I had to have his story. I needed it. When he finished I asked him, and he looked at me quizzically, as if he didn't understand.

"What about our pact?"

"Let it go," I answered. "I want to know you before you leave."

That was when I learned he'd been raised in a house where language was at cross purposes. His Spanish mother spoke with all the heightened rhetoric of her people, and her words grated against his father's pragmatism. By the time he enrolled in the university the conflicting claims of his divided blood were apparent. His course in literature distanced him even further from his father's world. He fell in love with young women and symbolist poetry, discovered Baudelaire and felt, for the first time, the attractions of the life of the flaneur, the man who looks on the passing scene while holding himself aloof. His mother's language had paved the way toward a romantic view of life that could not have been further from the business of his father's bank, but he was not strong enough then to ignore tradition, and he entered the firm where he spent two painful years before walking away from his ledgers in the middle of the day, deaf to his father's shouts as he pushed through the glass doors to freedom.

The money from a family trust allowed him to follow his whims. He lived in Vienna for a year, then moved on to Rome and London, during which time he wrote an unpublishable novel composed of pastiches of Goethe and Novalis. Soon after he arrived in Paris his renewed interest in Baudelaire gave birth to Heinz. He wrote *Dawn* quickly, but he was uneasy because he knew the voice was not his own. "I had only one subject, and one voice to describe it," he said. "I acquiesced, hoping something else would come along, but that didn't happen for years."

He met St. Omer, and with his help found an apartment on the Rue Littré, just off the Rue de Rennes and within easy reach of the bistros on the Boulevard Montparnasse. Every morning at six o'clock he rose to the sound of his alarm and spent the day wandering the streets of Paris and writing in cafés. He met Fabien soon after *Dawn* was published and they married a year later. It was painful to hear him talk about it because they were clearly unsuited for each other. She had been unhappy with the pattern he set upon his days from the beginning, and after two acrimonious years they divorced. "You know the rest," he said. "I'm afraid I've disappointed you."

It was not a remarkable story, but I was touched by his honesty and especially by the conflict that had lived so long in his divided blood, which even then he was trying to reconcile in the composition of his *Letters*. I admired his determination to change the direction of his life, but admiration strikes me now as a code for the feelings that had been pressing against my need to remain aloof for so long. When I gave in the Men in the Clock began tapping at the window to remind me that I had no power over them equal to Joaquín's when he turned away from Heinz, and for a while the ugly face of jealousy threatened to show itself because I passionately wanted Joaquín's freedom.

I paid a heavy price for his story. What began as a need for words to remember when he left took on a life of its own that I had no way of predicting. I had wanted something that would be the equivalent of the olive pits from Fuente Grande. Instead, I discovered a desire to meet him on an equal footing, as man and woman, even if it was only for a few months.

For two weeks I fought the Men in the Clock, who entered my thoughts with sickening regularity. Sometimes they spoke alone, sometimes together, as in a chorus. In the morning, while Claude and Monika ate a hurried breakfast, they sat across the table staring at me smugly, saying I was nothing but a fraud. When Joaquín and I were alone they rose from the pages of my books. "Give it up," they said. "What right do you have to want what you want?" "Every right," I answered. "You happened long ago, in another country. I used you to save my daughter's life." "They all had stories," they said. "All the whores at the Seven Dolphins. You were a *whore*, Ursula. Remember what you did? How you gave your body like a hollow gourd for us to fill time and time again? What do you think he would say if he knew?" "He would understand." They laughed. "You would disgust him," they said. "He would vomit at the sight of you."

It was like that every day. Had I been alone, I could have raged against those men who carried my past into the apartment like a chalice to be drunk from by demented priests. I could have thrown cups and dishes, shouted that guilt was not a birthmark to stain me until I died. But I was never alone. I was a mother, a mother-in-law, a companion to Joaquín. A social being woven into the lives of other people. There was no one to confide in, not even Madeleine. The slightest thought of revealing how I'd lived made my throat constrict until I feared I'd strangle on Berlin. The double life I'd had since Monika and I came to Paris seemed paradisal after Joaquín took refuge with us. Before it happened, deception was as easy as silence. Now silence was painful as a burn. Outwardly I played my role. Inwardly I listened to my visitors, shrank from their attacks, tried to avert my mind's eye from scenes held up like scientific proofs of why Joaquín and I would never look at one another with innocent eyes.

What happened then seems hardly different from what occurs in war. I retreated deep into myself, seeking the safety that the road offers to refugees. Days passed when I'd scarcely speak to Joaquín or the children. I concluded that I'd made a terrible mistake in letting down my guard. That it would have been better if I'd never entertained the notion that Joaquín and I might be something more to each other than the ciphers I'd demanded. That I'd been right to turn away from him when he appeared spattered with blood.

But one day, when bitter cold frosted the windows with patterns like broken glass, I realized that I was neither beyond redemption nor doomed to choke on my emotions. Like a herald, the idea summoned the Men in the Clock who rushed into the room banging cymbals and playing crazy melodies on wooden flutes. They were all there. Every man who paid for me was in that delegation, and for the first time I saw discomfort in their eyes, even glimmerings of fear. In response, and with mighty injured dignity, they took me up the stairs and made me watch what they had done. I knew it was coming, had known from the moment I understood that I was not doomed. This journey up the stairs of the Seven Dolphins was the price I had to pay, and it made no difference. Until that moment I thought their hands and tongues and swollen penises had paralyzed me. Now I knew that I could move, that all along the sickness of my heart had been my doing and not theirs. They could hold memory up until the room was as full of pictures as the Louvre, and I could stand it. I could live with what they showed me. I was alive again for the first time in twenty years.

That night was the first time I thought of my life as a map. I imaginatively put down everything with a steady hand, people and places, months and years, sketches of those who were dear to me. It was not a map where everything was there at once, as if from the day of creation. Time was part of it, and when I thought of myself I enclosed my figure in a circle to represent that stasis of my life, for I understood that I had moved through space, but not through time. Once Monika and I settled in Paris there was no more progress. I had some money from the Seven Dolphins, worked at various jobs, attended to her growing up. We lived frugally, but I wanted nothing for myself. I had had enough of Ursula Krieger, saw myself the way a banker sees bad debts. I existed for Monika, gave her all I could as she blossomed into womanhood.

I do not mean that I shrank from human contact. When the pain eased I wanted company. I found Pierre, a shopkeeper some years older than myself; Daniel, an accountant; Gerard, a translator at a small publisher. They slaked my loneliness at a distance because I could not truly be with them. Always the Men in the Clock appeared, and when they did my emotions washed up on the shore like something shriveled from the sea. I never reached fulfillment, and while it did not matter to me, my friends were always injured and left because I could not tell them why.

In the morning I resolved to enter time and leave some imprint on my map beyond the circle that had enclosed me. Cold seeped through the windows, and every sound that rose from the street seemed brittle.

Joaquín and I settled into the day's routine. I'd put on gloves against the cold, which made turning pages somewhat awkward. We were wrapped in old gray blankets that warmed us enough so that we didn't shiver, but my fingers were cold as ice. When he noticed my discomfort he said he'd make a fire in the kitchen stove. I told him we should save the paper until evening, but I quickly realized it was silly to endure the frigid air so I volunteered to make some coffee and a sweet.

As always, our paper logs were drying on the kitchen windowsill. They were uniform in size, about the circumference of a boccie ball, mottled in color, mostly gray, but here and there a strip of white or red or yellow showed. Every spare piece of paper we could find went into a pot of water until they were as soft as pasta. Our bookshelves were almost empty. Some of the logs were condensed novels or books of essays. Some were made up of tissue from boxes that once held presents, old issues of newspapers. Monika added to our hoard by stealing posters the Nazis plastered on walls announcing executions. The names of spies were usually listed on yellow paper with a black border. Terrorists, Resistance people and the like were assigned red posters with black borders. They sickened all of us to look at, but we were grateful for their warmth.

I usually managed to avoid reading the names, but the night before, my eyes had strayed to the yellow sheet before I dropped it in the pot:

1. Roger-Henri NOGAREDE de Paris
2. Alfred OTTINO de Saint-Ouen
3. André SIGONNEY de Oraney
4. Raymond JUSTICE de Oraney
5. Jean-Louis RAPINET de Pavillons-sur-Bois

A long paragraph of crimes followed, and there was a final comment that the men on the list were condemned to death by court-martial for aiding the enemy and taking part in Communist activities against the German army.

We burned only what we needed. When the food was cooked, the coffee made, the pathetically small pots of water boiled for sponge baths, we removed the logs from the stove, knocked the fire out, and put them on the windowsill to dry. The scent of burned paper inhabited the kitchen like a ghost, and had begun to reach into the other rooms as well.

While I measured out the water, Joaquín set fire to two half-burned logs. The gray paper reminded me of the names I'd read the night before and I busied myself, trying to forget. Monika had salvaged some singed baguettes from the bakery and I cut one in the middle, then divided the half loaf lengthwise. I placed the pieces on the stove and when they were toasted I sprinkled a little sugar on them and covered that with slices of withered apple.

The kitchen was so small that two people could not work without touching. Although we tried to avoid it, from time to time our hands made contact, or our shoulders, or sometimes our hips. When I removed the bread from the stove I wanted to put the sugar on immediately, and in my haste my breasts grazed his shoulder. He acted as if he hadn't noticed, but as soon as I looked at him I knew he wanted me. It was like the flaring of a match, but not the yellow fire that lies in the glances of men one passes on the street, or the gas-blue coldness of the Seven Dolphins' patrons. It had been there for three years, fixed in his irises as bright as a stone set in silver. The Men in the Clock revolved on their moving platform, but I turned away from them, telling myself to remember what I'd learned the night before, that there had been too much penance. I remember the wail of a siren coiling up from the street as he spoke my name and then, very gently, touched my lips. I was distraught and passionate at the same time, and it took a moment for him to understand whatever pain I felt was not his doing and that I welcomed his embrace. I led him to my bedroom. It was neat and spartan and the diffuse light from the frosted window cast the objects there in a warm, impressionistic glow. We were neither tentative nor hurried, and our lovemaking was as graceful as it was silent.

Afterward we pulled the blankets up and lay close together.

The unaccustomed warmth of another body seemed almost as voluptuous as our embraces. He worried that Claude or Monika might find us and I said that it would not kill them if they did. Then I put my hand on his chest. "You're still a mystery. I only know the man everyone knows. What do you dream about?" And that was when he told me what had happened after his visit to Fuente Grande.

He had returned to the hotel exhausted and angry, and after dinner he'd sat up a long time, thinking about what he'd seen.

"Sometimes," he said, "just before I fall asleep, I know what it is I'll dream. It was that way in Granada. I could have forced myself to stay awake and think of other things, but I chose not to. I wanted the dream, though I didn't know why.

"I remember walking through the countryside, searching for something. In a while I found myself on Archbishop's Road where I heard indistinct music, so faint I couldn't be certain of the melody, or the instruments that made it, but as I went along the sound resolved itself into a cante hondo. I heard a singer's voice, two guitars, and saw a circle of people surrounding the musicians. Lorca was there, the schoolmaster, the banderillos, others I didn't know. In my dream they did not suffer. They were free of death, Ursula, above or beyond what had happened to them.

"The singer was a slight fellow with a broad forehead, receding hair, eyes that were large and frank, and they closed when he reached the highest notes. His voice was deep and very pure and his hands moved in time with the music, almost as if they were guiding the notes.

"Lorca sang with him and took great pleasure in the music. When the song ended, he saw me on the path and motioned for me to join them. After I passed the pool of Ainadamar and reached the center of the grove I saw other musicians, five or six men with horns who suddenly struck up a tune not at all like the cante hondo. It was a sardana, a folkdance from the Costa Brava. Everyone gathered in a circle around the musicians and when we began to dance I noticed figures beneath the olive trees and knew immediately that they were Falangists. I tried to make Lorca and the singer look, but they shook their heads, insisting on the dance.

"I suddenly understood that it was Luis Valdés trapped behind the screen of olive branches, and that he was doomed to stay there, unable to invade our magic circle or hear the music. Only then did I find the rhythms and match my friends step for step. It was the strangest dream I've ever had, and comes back once or twice a month."

I remember wanting nothing more than to lie there and ponder the images he'd given me, but as soon as he finished he reached for my hand and kissed my fingers. I thought it was a prelude to more love, but when I turned to him I saw that wasn't what he wanted.

"Now yours," he said. "What comes to Ursula in the night?"

"Little things," I answered quickly. "Unimportant things. Nothing like your dreams."

"Then what about your life. Berlin?"

I felt my face die. There's no other way to say it. The name reverberated in the room, repeated itself in echoes that hung on the air as the Men in the Clock returned, so many I could not count them all. Cymbals and flutes played a counterpoint to the music I'd imagined as Joaquín spoke. Kurt, Erik, Helmut, others whose names I'd forgotten or never knew stared down at me, their lips pursed, speaking the word *Berlin* loudly, softly, with contempt and also with loving kindness. I turned away but Joaquín wouldn't let me go. When he tried to wipe my tears away I held his hands.

"Never ask about it," I said. "Promise now, this instant."

He nodded. My visitors turned away, pivoted out of the room with a whirling sound and the clash of cymbals, their expressions almost as benign as those of parents who've disciplined an unruly child. But it was more than that. Something fundamental had been demonstrated, a choice placed before me, as if they'd said I could have Joaquín, but always and only on the condition that he would come to me through them. I didn't care. If that was the lesson of their catechism, I'd follow it to the letter.

8

I see the day I took Joaquín into my bed as an island in time, the silence between tick and tock. When my visitors returned, they wound the mainspring tight and once again I heard the sounds of ratchets and wheels and familiar voices.

Much as they lorded their power over me, something had changed. I had learned I wouldn't die if I risked living, and that knowledge allowed me to recover from their catechism, though I was bruised from the encounter. It felt as if they'd reached inside my chest to squeeze my heart, but even that pain was instructive. I soon understood that the hand was neither a patron's of the Seven Dolphins nor some nightmare Mayan priest's, but only mine.

•

Joaquín would not accept imprisonment on the Rue de Seine. Not only did he insist on shopping in the Rue de Buci, but he also met with St. Omer to deliver the latest letter, or discuss plans for the next issue of *LER*. He knew it was foolish, knew that he should ration his forays into what he called the real world as stringently as we parceled out food coupons, but he had no choice. He had decided to live on the cusp of danger, as if that was the only way to repay the debt he'd incurred in Spain. Nothing I or the children said could persuade him otherwise, and ours were not the only warnings, for the German mania for precision had blossomed in the Nazis' minds. Informers and intelligence men penetrated more deeply than ever into the enclaves of the Resistance. When several members of the Lorca Club were arrested, men whose work had nothing to do with *LER*, the club disbanded, though Joaquín swore it was only temporary, and that they would reunite when the war was over. I was secretly pleased because it meant that he had one less risk to take, for he had insisted on going to La Masia every Saturday, if only for an hour.

After Feinstein was arrested in the spring and deported to a labor camp with a thousand other Jews, Joaquín spent a whole day away from the apartment meeting with St. Omer and representatives of clandestine papers in other cities. He did not tell me why. A week later he said that he was going away for a few days. "Where?" I asked. "The interior" was all he'd say.

I pleaded with him to be careful. It was bad enough when his restiveness took him to butcher shops and wine merchants, or when he met St. Omer, but I could endure such trips because they'd become familiar. I suppose it was his refusal to say where he was going, or why, that made "a few days" sound ominous. Precariousness ruled everyone's life, and I couldn't stand it any longer. I was irritable, self-absorbed, and without thinking I

asked, "What good will it do? You have the *Letters.*" "I can't
stay in the shade," he said. "You aren't. You haven't been since
Fuente Grande." "Remember Guernica?" he asked as he
glanced at his watch.

There was no point in arguing, so I said I'd see him off.
When we reached the foyer Madame Morain, the concierge,
opened her door. She was a harmless busybody who kept track of
everyone in the building. I'd told her Joaquín was a cousin from
Arles, a story we'd carefully concocted, and it had been the right
thing to say since she loved the town. She had a way of looking
at you over the top of her glasses that demanded an explanation,
and Joaquín obliged lightheartedly by saying that he was going
into the country to visit a friend who had a farm. Her eyes lit up.
"Does he have carrots? I'm expiring for the taste of fresh carrots." He promised to bring her some as he turned to me. "And
for my cousin, as well." He was going to leave me there, in
Madame Morain's care. I knew he was relieved that she'd cut off
the prospect of a private parting. I can't say I blamed him. I
expect I'd have made a final plea. Perhaps, God forbid, even
cried. I felt off balance, and his anticipation only made it worse.
It was the clearest indication I'd had that he needed to do these
things regardless of the cost, that whatever he'd been up to this
point in his life, now he was defined by risk. He leaned over and
gave me a very cousinly kiss on the cheek. "I'll see you in three
days." Then he was gone, and I had to pretend I wasn't worried.
As things turned out, there were reasons why I should have
been.

In his impatience to return from Lyons, for that was where
he'd gone, he neglected to ask certain questions about the safest
routes. Perhaps it would have done no good, since the Nazis had
discovered the virtues of unpredictability, but that oversight was
a signal, the first of several that changed the direction of his life.
I believe even more strongly now that he was destined for
Fuente Grande. In changing the direction he'd settled on to
repay the debt of Guernica, he chose what he thought was the

safe path, like a masked actor on the Greek stage who runs into his fate even as he flees it.

He had gone to Lyons with two men whose code names were Leconte and Jeannot. On the way back they took a train as far as a station some distance from the city, then switched to bicycles provided by Resistance men. It was late, they were in a hurry, and that was why he neglected to ask about the route they should have taken. They were stopped just outside the city limits at a checkpoint where an officer demanded their papers. The Resistance people had loaded their baskets with vegetables, and they told the Nazis they'd been out foraging for food. Joaquín said they knew a farmer, gave a name he'd made up on the spot. The officer examined their papers, and remarked that Joaquín was clean-shaven in his photograph. The officer questioned him about his name and Joaquín explained that he was German and had come to France when things were bad. He planned to return to Berlin when his wife recovered from a serious illness.

The officer returned his papers. It was clear that he wasn't completely satisfied, but a truck had pulled up belching smoke and he passed them through. When they were several hundred meters down the road Jeannot remarked that there was something on the officer's mind. He hadn't cared about him or Leconte, but he'd been suspicious of Joaquín. Joaquín had noticed it too, more closely than Leconte, but he rode in silence the rest of the way. He had carefully worked out several identities, had immaculate papers for each of them, but the one thing he couldn't disguise was his scar. It hadn't bothered him until then. Or, rather, he'd chosen to ignore it. On the ride back into the city he found himself thinking about it obsessively, and quite suddenly it seemed as visible as an arrow pointing to our building on the Rue de Seine.

I was frightened that night. As soon as it grew dark and he hadn't come back, I was convinced he'd been arrested. I felt torn between fright and grief, and I must have done something to make my consternation obvious because Claude came into the kitchen when I was preparing dinner and told me not to worry. There was a mischievous gleam in his eye which annoyed me. I'd begun seasoning our pathetic soup when Monika appeared and they smiled at each other. I saw her nod. "Ursula," he said, "the offer came."

I was furious. I asked what right he had to withhold the news, and he said it had only come that afternoon at the university. He'd been waiting for Joaquín, but when he saw how upset I was, he thought he should tell me.

I apologized and tried to get hold of myself. It was a shock. Since Claude had first mentioned the possibility I told myself we'd be in Paris for the duration of the war. I put away all hope of getting out because I was no good at hope, only endurance. Now it was real. I hadn't forgotten about Joaquín. If anything, I was more apprehensive, but I tried to distract myself by asking how long it would take to leave. Claude thought two or three weeks. Anything could happen in that time, I said, and no sooner had I spoken than Joaquín came in, looking shaken. I was so relieved that I jumped up and embraced him without a thought for how it looked. He was greatly pleased by Claude's news. "I'm glad," he said. "Now we can go together."

I sat there unable to understand his sudden change of heart. He and Claude agreed that two weeks was enough time to make the necessary arrangements and for him to finish the letters he had in mind. Claude had been making inquiries against the chance the offer would come. Friends had advised him that the best route was south, through Spain and Portugal, where we could take a ship from Lisbon. Now that Joaquín would be going with us his German citizenship complicated matters, but Claude said it would be possible to get a special visa for him at the American consulate in Marseilles.

That night I learned something new about Joaquín. He had been operating almost blindly, refusing to listen to St. Omer and others who counseled him to leave. He had refused to admit to himself that while we had accepted him with open arms, he'd put us in danger. He'd argued with St. Omer that his cover was still good, but now he understood his work had been achieved at the expense of reality, which had loomed up in the face of the Nazis at the checkpoint and in his thinking about his scar. He'd made mistakes he shouldn't have—had lived under the delusion of invincibility—and in doing so had lost the instinct to protect himself. It was a classic recognition, something the Resistance warned everyone about.

His ideas concerning the *Letters* underwent a change over the next few days. They would no longer appear in *LER*, but there were now almost enough for a book, and he could finish that anywhere.

I think it's predictable that the encounter at the checkpoint sparked his awareness. It happens with everyone who has been blind to things they should attend to. A slight shift in our angle of vision, an unaccustomed sound, a new texture reminds us of what we already know, but have been too occupied to understand. I'm surprised only that he ignored it for so long, because he was not foolhardy. I suppose his energy came from his fidelity to Lorca.

●

Once we committed ourselves to leaving we were more cautious than we'd been. The ruse of Joaquín's being a cousin from Arles had seemed fine at first, but I began to think I saw suspicious glances from other tenants. I was overly sensitive, afraid something might happen. I couldn't help it. It took all my strength to avoid thinking about disasters.

Monika, on the other hand, was happy as a lark. The idea of a new life in America excited her beyond bounds, and she talked about what it would mean to her photography, this chance to see with new eyes. There was an enthusiasm in her I hadn't seen since she was a girl in her teens, and it touched Claude, too. The depression that had settled over him with the Occupation had vanished, and he could be forgiven for being a little full of himself just then.

Despite my apprehension, I too was happy. For the first time in years I looked ahead, past the next day, though I was wary of naiveté. Until I saw gulls flying, until we actually embarked on the ship in Lisbon and a little distance opened between us and the dock, anything could happen. But I was thrilled by the prospect of never seeing Nazis again, of no longer having to endure the strutting music of noontime bands, of leaving behind the Men in the Clock. For that too was in the offing. I felt I had reached the threshold of change where the strands of my inner and outer life might be bound together again. I had told myself that Joaquín and I had come too late into each other's lives. When we made love the first time, I thought of it as a form of farewell, a parting gift to each other. But that had changed, and I, the seasoned skeptic, felt there was a chance for us in America. I imagined the view from the ship as it made its way across the sea. In its wake I saw my Men in the Clock drowning, and as they slipped beneath the waves my shame drowned with them.

Joaquín and I grew closer day by day. Sometimes, when his writing was done, we made love. I told him that his work was the most important thing, that there would be plenty of time for us when he finished. He laughed and said, "I thought you might expect me to perform like a youngster," and I told him that I wanted no young man.

The *Letters* were coming with incredible speed, and while they are all filled with insights about the twin conditions of Spain and Germany, the last one he wrote has a special eloquence, and I want to copy it out as a memento of those splendid days.

Listen to the Caudillo: "We have shot no poets."
Listen to the voice of the Falangist paper, *Unidad:* "I swear solemnly, by the friendship Lorca and I once shared, and by my blood shed in the noblest tempests of the battle-

field, that neither the Falange nor the Spanish Army had any part in Lorca's death. The Falange always forgives and forgets. He would have been our greatest poet, for his sentiments were those of the Falange: he wanted Fatherland, Bread and Justice for all."

After they killed him they realized their mistake. Lorca's riddled body did not rest comfortably in the rocky soil of Fuente Grande. Imagine their surprise when the questions came from all over the world. They thought they had killed a meddler, an apologist for the Reds, a spokesman for Gypsies. But Lorca rose up and walked abroad in the noonday sun. He sang from fountains, and was reflected in the moon. The bullets that passed through him sprouted wings and flew into the Caudillo's chambers, sucking out his peace of mind as easily as hummingbirds do nectar from a rose.

Consider this, and then think of how they tried to lie about his ghost. "He was one of us!" they exclaimed. "How could we kill our own flesh and blood, like the cannibal sow who eats her farrow?" The Caudillo's lie was meant to bury Lorca once and for all, his words to be heavier than the soil and stones already heaped on his bleeding body.

"We have shot no poets."

I ask you to imagine the Caudillo sitting ramrod straight as a journalist from Mexico asks if he is ready to begin. He nods, the reporter studies his notes, then glances up at Señor Franco.

"Have you shot any writers of world reputation?"

The Caudillo's men have arranged the interview for the sole purpose of allowing him to deny what the Falange had done. He has practiced his response with underlings in order to make certain that he says exactly the right thing to get himself off the hook. He has been looking forward to the end of this unpleasant business, which has embarrassed his cause and threatened his reputation. Yet, just before he answers, his authority asserts itself. He feels his strength, and even though he has agreed to the interview, his pride rebels and he thinks of removing his pistol from its polished holster and calmly shooting the reporter between the eyes. He imagines the clatter of the chair as the man falls backward, imagines the fan of blood and impudent brains, imagines replacing his pistol and turning calmly to his startled aides. The little dream gives him satisfaction. He could do it, but knowing that he could is enough and he leans forward stiffly, conscious of his military bearing.

Instead of shooting the impertinent reporter, he tells him there has been a lot of talk about the death of a poet encouraged by the Reds for propaganda purposes. He says that the poet was mixed up with the rebels in the early days of the revolution and that his death was one of the inevitable accidents of war. He hints vaguely that Lorca's death came at the hands of Republicans. He recites from memory the names of Nationalists killed by the opposition. Then he leans back, pauses, and says again, "We have shot no poets."

Why should it have mattered to him?

It mattered because Lorca was a poet who told the truth about the Spanish heart. Because he made unforgettable pictures of the truth.

How could it not have mattered after Lorca's portrait of the Guardia Civil as "humpbacked and nocturnal," scattering "fear like fine sand"? Or of their victim Rosa of the Camborios, who "sits groaning on her doorstep, her two severed breasts lying on a salver"?

It mattered because Luis Valdés oversaw the execution of a poet who preached not in bookish Latin but the language of the people, a poet whose altar was not marble and lace but rocky soil, and the Alhambra, and the Gypsy caves of Sacromonte.

The Caudillo swore he had shot no poets because he knew a sacrilege had been committed at Fuente Grande. The Falange had made the mistake Prince Hamlet refrained from when he came upon the fratricidal king praying in the chapel and thought, "Now might I do it pat, as he is praying; and now I'll do it—and so he goes to heaven." Unlike the melancholy prince, the Falange could not contain revenge, and because of that Lorca ascended to a place they could not reach—the Spanish soul.

So the Caudillo had to say, "We have killed no poets." His lie told a truth he could not foresee, that words are icons he could neither burn, nor melt, nor bury. It is the same with the Nazis whose antennaed vans prowl the streets of Paris feeling for the words on our radios, who infiltrate our networks and kill those of us who write for papers such as this. We are all poets to them, Decour, Feinstein, even writers of dull prose such as myself. They take us at our work, kill us on the spot, or in a public square, or in the basement of the building on the Rue des Saussaies. They think they make a silence with our deaths. They think they can say they have killed no poets, failing to understand that their lies and our deaths are guarantees of truth and life in the further words of those who take up our microphones and pens.

Remember this: Our strength is nowhere more apparent than when the Caudillos of this world and their Nazi brethren are forced to say, "We have killed no poets."

I have been looking ahead, gauging what remains to be explained against the days left on the crossing. The pages I have written lie curled together and rustle like dried leaves, the singular sound of my devotion.

When I began this work in Lisbon I had no idea of form. Images, voices, and feelings overwhelmed me, and it seemed quite enough to put them down as they came, without worrying about where they led. This afternoon, when I finished copying the letter, I walked a while to loosen the stiffness in my legs. As I circled the deck I realized that there is indeed a pattern in all

I've said, and that it has been rising to a turning point which coincides with Joaquín's journey to Lyons.

After he left, and I escaped from Madame Morain, I went upstairs. I am aware now that Joaquín and I were free during the time I waited for him, and for some days afterward. I mean our paths could have led in several directions because the future was still open, the way it is at the beginning of "Romance Sonámbulo." I was apprehensive, of course, and my uneasiness must have been no different from the Gypsy's as she watched her lover ride into the hills. Just as her thoughts traveled with the smuggler, so mine did with Joaquín. I forced myself to endure his absence hopefully, and declared the countryside free of threats to his safe passage. In this, I was like all who have found themselves within reach of their desire, whether it is love, as was the case with me, or wealth, or simply a plate of food. When hope becomes visible on the horizon we think of ourselves as following a path. Our minds fill with metaphors of travel, as if we were explorers who have wandered for years in deserts or sere countrysides who then suddenly see the perfect shape of our desiring, the best part of life, that which we were born for. So it was with me. When Joaquín returned, and I understood that we could leave together, I surpassed the Gypsy's hope. My desire was there before me, palpable and whole. At that moment it was inconceivable that it could be illusion, but it was, and I must return to the poem because the Gypsy's dream shows the true direction of what remains for me to tell, even to the point where she awakes to see nothing but the moon-flecked water of the pool below her balcony.

9

Over the next few days Claude and Joaquín made inquiries about ships in Lisbon and arranged to take the train to Marseilles where they would secure Joaquín's exit papers and our tickets from the company's office. When they returned we would pack our bags and leave for America. All that remained was to follow the path that had opened for us, and we did follow it, and there was no way we could have predicted the appearance of an obstacle that did not so much alter our direction as force certain changes in our plans.

To put it simply, there was a rat in the attic of our building on the Rue de Seine, one of a species that comes to life in dusty corners at times like those we lived in. Such creatures live dormant in out-of-the-way places until something like the Occupa-

147

tion happens, or a Franco comes to power. Then they stir from
their complacency, spring to life from paranoia, hatred, or the
chance of gain, and they always do so in the same way. The most
brazen speak themselves into the rat's life, open their mouths
and utter scandalous, dangerous words. The more timid find
scraps of paper, stubs of pencils, pens with frayed nibs, inkpots
with an eighth of an inch of ink half coagulated in the bottom.
Some speak only a single word, a name, a location. Others go on
until their throats are raw from the unfamiliar energy and their
lips sting with the taste of bile. Those in the brotherhood of rats
who distrust their voices write and write, as if language had only
recently come upon them. When the first scrap of paper is filled,
they frantically scurry about searching for others, and if nothing
comes to hand they will, in the heat of passion, dismantle a
picture frame to get at the photograph of themselves, or a wife
or husband, a mother or a father, a whole family. And they
continue writing on the back of the photograph. For however
long it takes, whether they write or speak, they are drunk with
the creative spirit, filled with the same impulse Lorca once attributed to a demon who freed his voice and gave him those
exquisite images.

Our rat lived peaceably in a small apartment on the top floor
of the building. His name was Guy Lafont. That was all I knew
of him at the time. Later, on the morning of our departure, he
left an indelible image on my mind, more powerful than anything that has ever come to me in dreams. I draw upon it now to
construct his history, use his startled, anguished eyes as goads to
my imagination, forcing from them details of a life that touched
us all. What follows is as true to his spirit as I can make it.

Lafont was, without a doubt, happy in his dormant state. For
years he had lived quietly and contentedly with his wife. Every
day he went to his job in Les Halles and worked eight or ten
hours, rarely grumbling and never really feeling discomfort for
what fate had given him in the way of a life. He was a man of
modest aspirations, content to trundle wheelbarrows and lift

boxes during the day, to eat his fill and then regularly join with his wife in quick, perfunctory intercourse which put him to sleep like a baby every night.

He was among the most comfortable of men, uninterested in the world beyond the borders of his daily existence. He had survived forty-eight years without ambitions of any kind, and sometimes he shook his shaggy head in disapproval at people scurrying to and fro on the streets, unable to understand why anyone would work, or even move, at anything other than a slow and calculated pace. He himself needed only enough food, enough wine, a warm place to sleep and occasional conversation with his colleagues at work, and less often with his wife, to be content.

But all that changed with the advent of the Nazis, though not immediately, because Lafont was slow in understanding the new. When anything out of the ordinary occurred he paused within himself and stared very much like a startled rat.

That happened after the Germans filled the streets of Paris and his apartment became so cold he could not maintain his bodily warmth. He paused and stared as the coal shuttle emptied, as the quality and quantity of his soup diminished, as his narrow circle of movement was curtailed.

Lafont had no opinion about the Occupation. The Nazis were simply there one day and, because of that, his life had changed. That was sufficient for him. He never felt the alteration on the surface of his skin, never realized that it was imperceptibly developing a soft, furry covering. All he knew was that the Nazis looked kindly on people with certain kinds of information. That money, coal and food might be exchanged for words. It was then that he took a new interest in the life of our building.

Apartments in Paris are no different from those throughout the world. One does not live in such a society long before discovering interesting things about the other tenants if he chooses. Until the Occupation Lafont lived complacently in our building, ignorant about the rest of us. But when his stomach began to growl, when his fingers were always cold and even the heat from Adrienne's body was not enough at night, he became attentive. At first it was merely out of curiosity to see if we suffered as he did. He felt a certain satisfaction when he discovered this was true, that even those in the larger and more comfortable apartments were cold and forced to scavenge.

Lafont felt no sympathy for any of us, though sometimes he liked to think of Monika naked on a bed. Whenever that happened, he tried to engage her in conversation. She was polite, nothing more, but any response was enough to arouse him. He would be especially urgent with Adrienne that night, and his eagerness perplexed her until she spoke of these occasions to other women, who told her that it was often the same with their men. She attributed these more passionate intervals in their usually perfunctory coupling to middle age and endured what he wanted with a certain curiosity.

His disdain for the rest of us turned to resentment when Joaquín appeared. He did not like the way he looked. He seemed too sure of himself, for one thing. For another, he was privileged, for he apparently did no work. This was corroborated by his wife, who said Joaquín was always there during the day, and when he did go out, it was usually only for an hour or two early in the morning.

So there was a certain logic in his attention to Joaquín, fueled by the occasion and a sense of injustice. Soon his nose twitched and he smelled an opportunity to make his life more comfortable. One night, after work, he told Adrienne to bring him a piece of paper and a pen. He sat before the sheet for a long time, for he had done no writing since leaving school except for chalking inscriptions on barrels in the warehouse. He fretted over how to begin and finally, after considerable distress, settled on something that seemed appropriate. He wrote a page describing his suspicions as best he could. Exhausted after spending an hour at the table, he fell into bed, but the demon was on him and he could not sleep. Whenever he closed his eyes he thought of other things to say. Three times in as many hours he got up and added to his letter. The next day, groggy from lack of sleep, he went to a stationer's and bought an envelope and stamp. He mailed the letter at the post office down the street from our building and on the way to work imagined a bouillabaisse, then a bowl of lentil soup filled with chunks of spicy sausage. He labored all that day in a happy frame of mind.

•

This imagined history of the rat in our attic sickens me not only because Lafont plays a role in what happened later to Joaquín, but also because there was such a rat in Lorca's life, the one who made the call to the Civil Government, saying that he had seen him at his father's house. All morning, as I wrote these pages, I have been thinking of the place Joaquín dreamed of for Lorca and all the others who had been taken to Fuente Grande. It is like a bubble in time, a place outside of, above, or beyond what we call reality. It seems very real to me, even more so now that I'm on my way to America. I see the place clearly, as completely as Joaquín described it, but my conjuring of Lafont has given me something besides the final reality of that place. Just moments ago, while I was looking at the sea, I saw a figure I did not recognize at first. Now I know it was Valdés.

He is smiling at what I say. It seems to be night there, and the firelight charges the olive groves with the color of old bronze, revealing Valdés moving from tree to tree, more than a specter, less than a man.

He comes as close as he can to the fire. I see him resplendent in uniform, intense as he was when Lorca and the others were brought to the Civil Government during those first months of the war and he drank cup after cup of strong coffee as he attended to the disposition of their souls. It was not good for him, for he suffered even then from the internal ailment that finally

151

killed him. I see Lorca standing by his desk as he drank, wincing with each sip as if he were hurting himself on purpose, causing himself pain so that he might be more ruthless.

He smiles at my story of the rat with eyes the color of obsidian stones set into a saffron face. His hair is slicked back, as it was in those days. His mouth is a thin, unarticulated line of malice as he stands beside a gnarled olive tree, hand to ear. As I described the rat in the attic he smiled with the pleasure of recognition, and I understand why that was so. Such creatures as Lafont crawled through the streets of Granada and Valdés knew how to feed them, bait their traps, coax them to his office with promises of rewards for their bits of paper or their words. He has enjoyed the story so far, and he will enjoy the rest of it too, for he must know what is going to happen, and that there was nothing we could do.

I feel certain that he knows the Marseilles train left the Gare de Lyon on Sunday morning, two days after Lafont mailed his letter to Gestapo headquarters. Claude had been granted a leave from his classes on the strength of a story he'd concocted about an ailing aunt in the southern port. They arrived in Marseilles, at the Gare St. Charles, around midnight and, since they were exhausted, they immediately took a taxi to a hotel Claude knew, the Grand Hôtel de Genève on the Rue Reine-Elizabeth, behind the Old Port.

Early the next morning they walked down the Canabière to the port where they had a wretched breakfast and watched hungover sailors making their way back to their ships after a night in the bordellos. It was a rough area, but Joaquín drank in the sights and sounds. Marseilles was nothing like Paris. It had an ambiance all its own, and he insisted that they stay awhile. At the Gare de Lyon the previous day he had suddenly become aware of how little time he had left in France, and now he wanted to savor everything he could. The white limestone hills surrounding the harbor were bright in the morning sun. He felt as if he were in another country. In a sense, it was true. Marseilles lay outside the occupied zone, and for a while he toyed with the idea of what life would have been like for all of us there. But the dream soon vanished when he thought of me. He understood at once that whatever troubled me had nothing to do with Paris, that I would have suffered in Marseilles, or London, or Rome. Claude was leaning back in his chair at the time, enjoying the warmth, when Joaquín found himself on the verge of asking him about my past. He refrained only because to press it with Claude would be disloyal to me, and he accepted my silence, though it persisted in bothering him throughout the day.

When Claude finished his coffee he stood up and said that since it was some distance away they should start for the consulate. He had no idea how long the procedure would take, but he hoped that they could book passage on the Lisbon ship before lunch and have the rest of the day to explore. Joaquín was looking at a freighter far out in the harbor and laughingly said to Claude that they would be lucky if their ship was in such good shape.

"What does it matter?" Claude said. "So long as it's seaworthy, and the captain knows his way to San Francisco."

There was anticipation in his voice, and Joaquín felt it too. Radical change was just ahead of them, and it was beginning to have a tonic effect, enough so that his sentimental regard for France faded away as he plied Claude with questions about San Francisco all the way to the consulate.

The diplomats were sympathetic. The man in charge, Chester Anderson, leafed through a file containing letters from Joaquín's sponsors, a group of American writers, as well as a few from scholars Claude had written to, asking for testimonials on Joaquín's behalf. Anderson asked to see Joaquín's German passport, which was essential for the visa. Everything was in order and he told them they were wise to leave while they could because no one knew when the Vichy government might close the border. He excused himself and returned half an hour later with their papers. Joaquín thought he was very efficient, and it seemed to him that he might very well like America. As they were leaving, Anderson asked about their plans. Joaquín explained that they were buying passage on a Portuguese ship from the company's office in Marseilles. Anderson reminded them that they needed Spanish tourist visas and Claude assured him that they would take care of that once they had the tickets.

Two hours later they returned to the hotel and Joaquín handed over the visas and tickets to the desk clerk who locked them in the hotel safe. Then they went out to find a place for lunch and discovered a restaurant not far from the hotel where they had a splendid bouillabaisse and shared a bottle of Montrachet. As they ate they felt the slight rocking motion of the ship in Lisbon harbor, saw the skyline beyond the Golden Gate, discussed the pleasures of San Francisco. Joaquín let his imagination linger on the pastel houses as he finished the last of his wine.

Claude wanted to stay in the port area, assuring Joaquín that it would be worthwhile.

"Trust me. There's something here well worth seeing."

Joaquín was willing to go wherever Claude wanted, so long as he could find a souvenir for Monika and me, something to mark the occasion.

Ten minutes later they were in the streets around the Porte d'Aix and the Rue Ste. Barbe. Men in dashikis, men turbaned and swathed in long black robes flowed by them on the sidewalks. Algerians, Tunisians, Moroccans jostled them, and the air was alive with a dozen tongues, as if they'd been set down in some forgotten corner of North Africa.

"Like it?" Claude asked.

"Of course. But it's completely unexpected."

They were accosted by the exotic scents of African food, of spices in open baskets which made the air redolent with their rich, pungent scents. They stopped in a shop whose contents were displayed on the sidewalk and, after much deliberation,

Joaquín chose two sets of earrings, very long but delicately worked, which he thought would please both of us.

"What now?" Claude asked. "I'm at your disposal."

The one place Joaquín had thought about on the way down from Paris was the Château d'If.

"Do we have time to visit Monte Cristo's chambers?"

"I should have guessed. Of course. Monika and I went there a few years ago."

•

Although mail was irregular, and letters often went astray for weeks, Lafont's envelope arrived at Gestapo headquarters on Monday morning, just as Claude and Joaquín left the restaurant for the consulate, a little before I saw Monika off for her day at the bakery.

There were well-established procedures on the Rue des Saussaies for communications like Lafont's. It first came into the hands of a portly sergeant recovering from a night on the town. He had drunk too much wine, and his pipe tasted foul as he opened the envelope, squinting to read the awkward phrases and decipher the crude innuendos. It was difficult to concentrate because of his hangover and also because he had been thinking of his wife in Munich. He was afraid that she had become enamored of a butcher on their block, but his jealousy was lessened a little as he remembered with satisfaction the woman he had been with the night before. Only after resolving his domestic problems did he return to the letter and, recognizing that it fit a category that had been drummed into him, put it into the hands of his assistant to deliver upstairs.

What with delays of one kind or another, it was almost noon before the letter made its way through two intermediate stops and reached the desk of Obersturmführer Gerhard Munch. He was a tall, sandy-haired man whose face revealed nothing of his feelings. During the occasional moments of introspection he al-

lowed himself, he was sometimes willing to admit that his career
owed as much to his expressionless face as to his mind, and this
always made him uncomfortable. He disliked the idea of chance,
preferring to think that everything happened through rational
cause and effect. Nevertheless, he took very good care of his
face, lavishing fine soaps and oils on it, as if he were an actor of
some renown.

Munch read the letter quickly because his aide had delivered
it just as two of his superiors arrived to take him to lunch. They
were going to a café rumored to have excellent rouladen, and so
food was paramount in his mind as he scanned the accusations
above Lafont's awkward but ostentatious signature. He suspected its veracity from the first line. Letters arrived from
known informers every day, and many more from aspirants like
Lafont who couldn't conceal their hope of gain. Although the
letters often provided excellent intelligence, and scrutinizing
them was integral to his job, Munch decided to put off thinking
about it until after lunch. He had not recognized Lafont's name,
and he had no desire to make a fool of himself as he had done on
several occasions recently, wasting time and resources on false
allegations. Besides, Lafont had been exceedingly vague in his
accusations. As Munch rose and buttoned his jacket he was in-
clined to dismiss the letter as nothing more than an attempt at
petty vengeance. The French were increasingly forced to live
with each other for a variety of perfectly innocent reasons.
There would be time to consider what to do later in the afternoon.

As Munch left with his colleagues Lafont pushed a wheelbar-
row through the warehouse and whistled a fragment of a popular
song whose name he did not know. His normally lackadaisical
pace had quickened, and there was even a glint in his eyes as he
thought of a lentil soup filled with greasy sausages. Then he
remembered the way Monika's bottom looked in a tight skirt.
He was, he realized, happier than he had been in months.

It must have been about that time when I finished shopping

on the Rue de Buci where I had bought some pathetic vegetables I intended to use in a ratatouille that afternoon. The sidewalk was icy, and I walked carefully. The cold came through my thin coat but it did not matter. I had been excited all morning thinking about Claude and Joaquín in Marseilles. I even allowed myself the luxury of wondering what the ship would look like. The closest I had ever come to one were the wooden sailboats Jürgen used to play with in the parks, and I remembered that they always seemed precarious and fragile as the wind took them on their haphazard journey across the pond. I had never seen the ocean either, but the idea of crossing it was easy to visualize. I knew how it would feel, how the ocean would look, and I was trying to imagine the effects of a storm when three Nazi officers stepped out of a sedan and headed in my direction. When they were close I stepped aside. Usually I hated giving ground, but that day things were different. I actually enjoyed making way because I wanted to concentrate on seeing them pass out of my vision. It was a game I spontaneously devised, a preparation for what would happen very soon. But I did not get far enough away. There was ice on the curb and I was forced to stop short of it, afraid that I might slip if I went any farther toward the street. The nearest officer brushed against my shoulder and I said "Pardon," but he ignored me. They were talking about lunch, and I was no more important than a lamppost.

Normally I did not think about such insulting behavior, but this was different. As the Nazi passed I caught the scent of his cologne. It meant nothing for a moment, and then I recognized it as the same as a patron of the Seven Dolphins wore, a government official who always chose me. I went on, determined to forget, but the visitor stayed with me as I hurried down the street, no longer mindful of the ice. The clock struck faintly then, and several of my familiars looked down and smiled as if they were standing on the deck of the Lisbon ship. It took all the discipline I was capable of to force them from my mind, but I was determined that they would not spoil the day. I imagined working in the kitchen, making the ratatouille, and by the time I was home and had closed the door all that remained of the incident was the vague scent of bay rum.

In the meantime Munch had forgotten about Lafont's letter. After he returned from lunch, stuffed with roulades and a little hazy from two glasses of wine, he saw it lying in a wire basket. He put his feet up on the desk and admired his boots. The letter made him feel ill at ease and, while he was obliged to make a decision, he consciously put off picking it up. Only a few weeks earlier a similar letter had arrived and he had made a fool of himself when his men returned and told him that they had found no trace of the incriminating evidence the writer so confidently assured him was there. His instincts told him that was very likely the case with this Guy Lafont. If it was, he would make an example of him.

By then the pleasure of lunching with his superiors, both of whom had complimented him on his work, had been lost in his anger toward Lafont. With a sigh he reached for the letter and read it slowly, several times. The man was barely literate, and Munch laughed out loud at his prose, which was both flowery and crude. The sentences, written in a childish scrawl, were fawning one moment, comically arch the next. But he was interested now. The habits of the man Lafont identified only as the newcomer in Number 12 were just odd enough to pique his curiosity. He read it over again, and this time he could not deny that there might be something to the accusations. It was better to risk another wild-goose chase than to miss the chance of snagging someone in the Resistance, or another kind of troublemaker. He thought of the impression he would make if this man in Number 12 turned out to be someone important. He felt a little flutter of pleasing vanity, and that was when he decided. In a swift, elegant movement he swung his chair to the left of the desk and his boots hit the floor with a crisp, satisfying sound.

"Manheim!" he called, and his aide scurried into the office.

10

Ten of them made the trip in a motor launch to the rocky island. As soon as they landed, the guide, a young man with a scrawny beard, began his recitation. Claude whispered that they might as well submit to the obvious, but Joaquín did not know the history of the Château d'If and listened attentively to the guide explaining that the castle had been built in the sixteenth century as a defense against invaders, and only years later, when it was no longer needed in that capacity, had it been turned into a state prison. "As some of you may know, the most famous guest at the château was Alexander Dumas's Count of Monte Cristo. Dumas was very precise in his descriptions. There will be time to show you the cell, and the passageways he wrote about."

○

The stones had weathered with the dignity of great age and the group's footsteps echoed insignificantly as they made their way to the famous cell. Joaquín was struck by how bizarre it was. Only hours ago he had arranged to go into exile. Now he was a tourist. The sense of precariousness that had prompted the trip to Marseilles faded as they entered the dark corridors, replaced by an unfamiliar sensation he could not define except that he knew it was somehow connected with the restricted space. He reminded himself that he was not claustrophobic and tried to forget it.

The count's cell did not impress him. It was, after all, only the source for Dumas's tale. Claude, on the other hand, inspected every nook and cranny with his scholar's eye, and left only when the guide insisted.

Joaquín was more interested in the cells where Huguenot prisoners had whiled away the time carving images of themselves and their homes into the rocks. He studied the figures carefully and then, without warning, he felt the sense of oppression return so strongly that he could not ignore it. He left the cell, thinking that might help, but it did not. A premonition had come upon him that I was in distress, and it was only because the idea seemed so preposterous that he said nothing to Claude when they reached the top of the stairs leading to the battlements. There, looking back at Marseilles, he felt it as strongly as he had in the castle. He glanced at his watch. Hours remained until the train left for Paris. Since nothing could be done, he tried to convince himself that it was only the closeness of the walls, the echoing footsteps in the narrow corridors, his own precarious situation which made him susceptible to such intimations, but the feeling persisted.

●

I was standing in the kitchen, dicing vegetables. By some minor miracle I had found eggplants, as well as peppers and onions.

The scent of bay rum faded against the stronger earthy smell of the vegetables. I was determined that the encounter with the Nazis and the memory of the Seven Dolphins would not ruin the afternoon. I concentrated intently on making perfect geometrical forms of the vegetables. It seemed, at the same time, as if I were physically holding my consciousness at bay, forcing it to remain in the present.

As I sliced the onions I looked up and there, in the kitchen window, the Men in the Clock buzzed like flies at the frosted glass. I brandished my knife threateningly, told them to be wary, warned them that things had changed and now they were small enough to dispatch. They buzzed, their tiny bodies tapping ineffectually at the window. Then they were gone. I remember smiling, being aware of a strange new certitude that had come upon me when I knew we were leaving. I ignored all the warnings I had so carefully made, forgot all the pitfalls I had conceived of. As I finished preparing the dish I mused about gardens in the state of California. Claude had assured me that it was a place with a temperate climate, like Provence, and as I covered the pot I thought of long hot days in the sun, of the rows of vegetables I would grow in my garden. In my mind I had already left France. I refused to accept the cold, the fact that my hands ached from the icy water I had plunged them in to prepare the food. My fingers looked raw as I dried them and it did not matter. Then I went into the living room where I wrapped myself in my old gray blanket. I was thinking about Joaquín, about the *Letters*, and decided that it would be interesting and appropriate to reread the novels of his now defunct quartet, to have that experience again and leave the world of Heinz behind with everything else. I would read the accumulated *Letters* on the way out of France, on the train. That too would be appropriate. I felt stronger than I could remember, victorious in some tender, new way.

And it was then, in the midst of that unfamiliar sense of power and well-being, that it all unraveled. Actually, as it seems

161

to me now, it happened approximately half an hour earlier when the two Mercedes sedans left Gestapo headquarters at just about the same time Joaquín and Claude boarded the motor launch for the return to the mainland. There were seven Nazis in those cars, three officers and four soldiers. Munch and Manheim sat in the back seat of the lead car, neither very excited about what they were doing. "But you never know," Munch said reflectively. "There is enough so it's prudent to take a look."

When I heard the car doors slam in the street I knew they were Nazis. The French, except for collaborators, were no longer permitted to drive. Voices drifted up from the street, but they were too faint for me to make out the words. Then there was the sound of boots on the stairs and soon they were coming along the hall. There was just enough time to wonder who might have attracted their attention when the knock sounded. Not until then, not one instant before, did I think they were coming to our apartment. Does that sound impossibly naive? All I can say is that the fear we'd responded to was generalized, a reaction to the overall conditions, not the displeasure Joaquín had caused with his *Letters*. That, I think, is what must have gone through my mind. But now, from the vantage point of the deck, with nothing but an uninflected sea to gaze upon, I know how I deceived myself. I did not think they were coming to our apartment because I could not allow such a notion into my consciousness. We had gone too far, all of us, and I realize that my earlier caution, my hedging of bets, had been merely rhetorical and I'd never truly believed it. But reality returned with the knock, that one-toned, dry announcement that my integrity was about to be violated, that my place in the world, our family's place, would be deformed into shapes that were still unimaginable. It was, in an instant, a summons and a judgment upon my recent naiveté. I had been reading *Dawn*, but I had also been thinking about the *Letters*, so it was no great feat of imagination to see Lorca looking up, startled and afraid, when the Falangists came to the Rosaleses' house.

I opened the door and found myself staring at the officer who had brushed against me on the Rue de Buci. The scent of bay rum was overpowering. He wore round silver-rimmed glasses now that gave him an abstract, scholarly air. I almost laughed at the coincidence. Perhaps I should have, as things turned out. It might have unsettled him for a moment and changed the direction of his thought, altering what followed. But I was too surprised. He knew it, too, because he stood there without saying a word, as if he were taking my measure for pliancy, veracity, fear, God knows what else. The light reflected on the lenses of his glasses so that I could hardly see his eyes as he looked at me and then beyond into the living room. He did this slowly, with considerable deliberation, and I knew he was expert in reading faces as well as objects that lay about in rooms. Then he glanced at me again. His almost casual, insolent expression hardened as his face filled with knowledge until I was almost convinced he knew everything about me, even that his cologne had brought back the memory of my official whom I had christened Number Eleven.

"There is a man staying here who arrived a few months ago," he said casually. "I want to know who he is." With that he pushed the door open and came inside, followed by the others.

When we decided to shelter Joaquín we had anticipated a moment such as this. Unlikely as it was, we agreed that we must be prepared because life in Paris had reached the point where anything could happen. Nothing was beyond contingency. For several nights after dinner we created a new life for Joaquín, a new history, going around the table and exchanging ideas almost as if it were a game. We transformed him into a watchmaker whose business had fallen on hard times, and since I had given him my father's profession, I also made him a relative, a second cousin from Arles. We even invented alternative habits and gestures, which we forced him to try out until he was comfortable with them.

As soon as Munch asked his question I began my recitation,

calmly telling him about my poor and befuddled cousin, matching Munch's insolence with as casual and slightly aggrieved a tone as I could devise. Not once did I look away from his frank and probing eyes. I even managed to enforce my story with a certain intimacy just this side of coquettishness. I did so deliberately, calculatedly, and as the story unfolded I felt the enormous differences between us, not only because they were Nazis, but even more because they were men who made me feel as utterly alien and jeopardized in my femaleness as I had been in the days when I plied my trade at the Seven Dolphins.

Munch listened carefully. His intelligence was apparent as he probed with his eyes, listening for one false note, one single hesitation. I have had reason to think of him long and hard, have become very intimate with Gerhard Munch. Although I despised him, I admired his abilities. He knew exactly what to attend to. Verbal tics and the gestures accompanying lies were the subject of his expertise, as well as things I have never allowed myself to dwell on, the more brutal ones that Valdés made famous with his paseos. As I talked he looked around the apartment and then suddenly turned back to me without giving any indication that he would do so. I knew he was scanning my face for clues and also that he found none. Even before I finished he was convinced that this visitation only repeated the embarrassing situation he had found himself in recently. Because of that he bore down on me a little more with quick, pointed questions. Still satisfied that I was telling the truth, but concerned that his men might disparage his attentiveness if he broke off, he ordered them to search the rooms.

As they turned out drawers and cupboards he sat in my chair and flipped through the books stacked beside it. When he picked up *Dawn* I stiffened, but he did not look at the cover. I think it must have been at about that time he decided that I was interesting, and that he began thinking about my calmness. In that instant he also decided that something was not right. There was nothing he could put his finger on, nothing I said, nothing in my face, no gestures that betrayed anything other than a straightforward accounting of the truth. But something struck him, and he felt that he had to cover himself by taking me back to the Rue des Saussaies where, in the comfortable surroundings of his office, he would have a greater opportunity to talk more about this man who had gone to visit an infirm relative in Marseilles. After all, unexpected things happened with some frequency in his office.

"You will come with us," he said and, as if to emphasize his decision, he closed *Dawn* with a snap.

"But we've done nothing," I protested. "We're simply trying to live."

He was standing then, looking down at me.

"I am not charging you with anything, not yet," he said almost apologetically.

He motioned to one of the soldiers who came over and took me by the arm. He had a narrow, pallid face, pale blue eyes, a shock of straw-colored hair visible beneath his helmet. He frightened me. I don't know why, but I instinctively pulled away, and that was when he slapped me. My ears rang, and even though it hurt I managed to look at Munch with as much injured innocence as I could muster. He stared at me calmly. "Do as he says," and then they led me out the door. On the way I reached up and felt a cut beside my eye. The blow had bent the frames of my glasses, and when I took them off everything was hazy, so I bent them as straight as I could on the way down the hall and put them back on.

There was a certain ritual to my abduction which I know was calculated. They hurried me down the hall, one soldier on each side, Munch and Manheim leading the way. We passed Madame Lafont on the stairs, who took in the situation with a glance and seemed to melt into the wall as she made way. On the ground floor Madame Morain poked her head out the door and withdrew immediately, like an old turtle going back into its shell.

If I hadn't been so apprehensive, I think I would have attended more carefully to the strangeness of the situation, to the new, unexpected perspective which driving in a German car gave me. But I saw enough. Everyone on the streets noticed us as we went by, and their fear was evident. It was almost like a dream, as if I were seeing myself being looked at. I did my best to stay calm, and as carefully as I could I went over everything I had said to Munch, for I knew he would try to catch me in contradictions. The problem with lies is that since they have no specific gravity they refuse to stay in the mind with the solidity of actual events, floating off by themselves almost as soon as they are spoken.

Once we arrived at the Rue des Saussaies the little dance began, the minuet of cat and mouse Munch must have played with dozens, if not hundreds of Parisians. As we entered his office he motioned for me to sit down and then left without a word. For ten minutes I expected him back momentarily until I realized he was giving me time to lose my concentration, confuse my story. I was positive that was his intention.

Some papers were piled on a small table next to me, and while I had absolutely no interest in the so-called news, I thought, This will upset him, turn the tables. It will be the last thing he'll expect.

I slid down in my chair, propped my feet up on the table, and gave myself up to the collaborators' news. In doing so I regained some of my confidence because I had discovered Munch's intentions. It must have shown in my face as well as my slovenly position when he came in abruptly half an hour later, stopping just inside the door and looking at me as if he were uncertain what to do. We were dancing together then, formally, precisely, though the music we heard could not have been more different. He smiled, as if to say he understood that I understood. Then he took the paper from me, saying, "This isn't a social call." As soon as he sat down beside me he crossed his legs and began interrogating me like a priest intent upon the catechism. In the next fifteen minutes he put all the questions to me that he'd asked in the apartment, but with different emphasis, and I responded flawlessly. With each answer I felt more confident until it seemed that I could go on with Joaquín's story in my sleep.

Finally he tired. I could tell he was frustrated and thought that I'd be allowed to leave. Instead he touched the place where the glasses frame had dug into the skin around my eye. "That doesn't look good." He called to one of the men in the outer office, told him to find a bandage. The aide returned with one a moment later and Munch took it, handing it over very courteously. "You may use the lavatory in there to freshen up, if you like."

Our positions were reversed. I had had the upper hand when he first returned. Now he did. As I washed the wound and fixed the bandage I was aware that nothing was what it appeared to be.

"That's better," he said when I returned. The sharp tone of his interrogator's voice had been replaced with soft, cultivated syllables that were undeniably pleasing. He was a chameleon of many faces, tones, gestures, and I could do nothing but sit there, waiting to see who he would become this time.

"I believe you, Frau Krieger. At least to the extent that you are free to go in a while. But first you must tell me a little about yourself. We are both Germans. You came here years ago. Why?"

I told him that I had grown up in Berlin, and to put him off the track, I spent some time talking about my life with Hans. He was surprisingly sympathetic. To this day I do not know with any certainty whether it was genuine, or simply another ruse. In any case, he had lost an uncle in the war, and close family friends as well.

"Things were very grave afterward, I remember, though I was fairly young at the time," he said. "People had difficulties making ends meet. What did you do?"

I believe it was an innocent question, a natural question such a man would ask either from curiosity or with the subtle intention of filling out the dossier he was compiling in his head. I should have anticipated it as soon as he began probing into my past, but I did not. When it came, I had to exert every bit of self-control to avoid revealing my distress. It was not a matter of my personal safety, or of giving away anything that might harm Joaquín. Only my interior balance was at issue, what remained of the well-being I had begun to feel. I was tired by then, stripped of reserves, and I suppose it would have been odd if I had not had a fleeting glimpse of Old Berlin in all his disheveled glory. So I looked at Munch frankly and said that yes, times had been difficult indeed and I had made my way as well as I could. I said that I took in washing, that I cleaned, and then, because I could think of nothing more original, I said that I had been a waitress in the district of the Seven Dolphins. "Please," I added, "this has been very tiring. May I leave?"

It seems to me that Munch had been listening only half-heartedly until I mentioned my fictitious job. I think that re-counting Hans's death had actually struck a sympathetic chord, and he allowed me to go on out of a certain consideration for what I'd suffered. But when I mentioned the name of the district, his taciturn expression changed. It was not a smile but a tightening of his features, a sudden interest that I observed as he removed his glasses and laid them on the desk.

"Ah, yes, the street of whores."

Nothing remained of the scholar's appearance, but I was not surprised. My memory was open to the long-gone days of the Seven Dolphins when I had seen that change often enough never to forget it. I had always hated the moment when my patrons removed their glasses and placed them carefully on the table beside the bed. It was like an announcement, a sign that I could not escape, and that was how I felt with Munch. The scholar gave way to the lazy sensualist.

"Yes," I answered after a pause, "there was that."

He must have known I was lying about the café. What else could account for the change of expression, or the way he looked at me so candidly? I suppose that since he'd found no flaws in my story about Joaquín he may have felt resentful that he'd appeared a fool and this was his revenge. But that could not account for the way he looked at me as he slowly opened and closed the earpieces of his glasses. He made no attempt to disguise the course his eyes slowly took from my face to my breasts and the fold of my skirt between my thighs. He was looking through my clothes as frankly as any of the patrons at the Seven Dolphins ever did when, wearing far less, I had waited in the parlor for them to choose.

"You never thought of joining them?"

"What?"

"You must have made very little as a waitress. A woman like you could have remained quite busy. You could have earned enough to come out well, despite the inflation."

He paused just long enough to gauge my response. I felt myself blushing and there was nothing I could do to stop it. "Enough to leave Berlin," he added, smiling.

I think now that he was fishing, indulging a streak of cruelty. But then I had no time to think. I was all feeling, nothing more. My face was hot from shame, from a sense of defeat as deep as any I have ever known. The cut on my cheek ached, and I heard a sound inside my head like a scream raised at the indecency of what he was doing. It was like rape, and the outrage and helplessness I felt would have matched any woman's as she was being violated.

"You have no right!" I shouted. "How can you say that?"

He was calm and deliberate.

"This is very interesting," he said, letting the ambiguity hang in the air between us for a moment before adding, "and I have all the right I need."

A kind of recognition appeared in his eyes, which were glittering now with something he intended to keep to himself. He was smiling, as if to fully establish his authority.

"To do this?" I asked. "Insult me like this?"

"Every right, Ursula. To do anything I like."

It was a terrible moment. I did not know what he was going to do when he suddenly rose from his chair. I was prepared for him to cross the room, shut the door, accost me, but he remained there looking down at me and then, with a decisive movement, picked up his glasses and put them on. He was satisfied. For a moment I think I almost wished he had come for me rather than savoring what had happened between us like a voyeur. For reasons I will never understand, his pleasure, his need had been satisfied in letting me know that he knew.

"Get out," he said suddenly, and then turned away to look out the window. It was snowing lightly and I ached to be in it, to feel it on my hands and face. I left without a word. Manheim glanced up from his work as I approached, looked beyond me into Munch's office, and then bent forward as if I were not there.

11

Lafont ate his bread and cheese standing beside a barrel near the loading dock. The bread was reasonably fresh, but the cheese was hard and cold. The slight astringency suggested it was on the verge of going bad. He would have a word with Adrienne when he went home. Old cheese was intolerable, and he wondered why he should be forced to eat such things when those with more money did not have to. He thought about the apartment building. From time to time, savory smells of cooking rose from the lower floors to his living room. He decided that they came from our apartment, and made rapid calculations in his head. It seemed indisputable that there had been an increase of such delicious odors at about the time the man came to live

171

with us. He was sure of it as he gnawed his hard cold cheese and sipped his wine.

Then his mood changed. He had forgotten that his fortune was on the mend. Vautrin approached and Lafont smiled, clapped him on the shoulder and said, "What about a drink later on?" suggesting that they go to a little bar not far from the warehouse.

After work Lafont waited outside the loading area. He was about to give up and go to La Belle Reine by himself when Vautrin came out, carrying his lunch bucket. He seemed surprised to find Lafont waiting.

"I thought you were joking."

"Not at all. Let's go."

After two cognacs Lafont's wallet looked very empty. He usually drank beer, but payday was not far off, and it was important not to drink alone when one had something to celebrate.

"Drink up! There's more where that came from."

He called to the waiter and ordered two more cognacs. He had been coming to La Belle Reine for years, and knew Pierre as well as anyone except his wife, but he adopted a formal air as he ordered, called Pierre Monsieur, and even Vautrin, who was not attentive to niceties of behavior, thought it very strange that Lafont was acting like a gentleman.

When Pierre brought the cognacs Vautrin put his elbows on the table and looked frankly at Lafont, who was positively brimming with confidence.

"Come on, Guy, out with it. You've never stood any of the fellows drinks before. Did a rich uncle die? Are you getting into somebody's pants? Marie's, maybe?"

Marie was the foreman's secretary and caused pleasant agony among the workers who fantasized about her sex life every day.

"Not at all. A man takes care of his affairs and things turn up."

In his mind Lafont had already received a generous gift from the Germans. He wanted to tell Vautrin about it, but he was not quite certain he would understand. He was pleased with his perspicacity, his innate ability to make such distinctions. It would be better, more discreet, to let him wonder. He glanced at Vautrin then, aware that he had risen in his colleague's eyes, that he was a presence.

"Things turn up," he repeated as he tossed off the cognac. He felt very good when he stood up and pulled out his pocket watch as he had seen one of the bosses do.

"I'm late," he said. "See you tomorrow."

Lafont was full of himself on the way home. He had definitely impressed Vautrin, and he congratulated himself for thinking about how the boss looked at his watch. It was the gesture of a busy man, an important man. On the métro he stood, even though there were seats, because that was the behavior befitting his new status. No more lolling about. He and Adrienne would have to go out more often, and not drink beer in public.

Lafont and I reached the building at the same time. I had walked most of the way in the hope that exercise would help me get hold of myself, but it hadn't done much good. It made no difference that Munch had intuited my past, or that, in doing so, he had asserted his power over me. Why should I have cared what he thought? But the effect of that long afternoon, the series of shocks and recognitions, left me despondent. Part of it had to do simply with the fact that the Nazis had been in our apartment, part with a renewed fear that they had come so close to finding Joaquín. But as I turned into the Rue de Seine, what affected me most was my own naiveté. I had thought I was breaking free from Berlin at last, from all that name conjured up. Now it was as if the last few weeks had never happened. The deepest effect of the afternoon was too strong to acknowledge fully, and I did what I could to make myself feel whole again, unviolated. I even tried to force myself out of that obscene grip of Munch's remembered expression to the place where I used to find the white dolphins, but it did no good. As I glanced at

Lafont who, at that time, was nothing more than a neighbor I rarely spoke to, I felt injured in my soul, felt my dignity in shreds.

He was looking at me intently. I realized that my eyes were probably still swollen from crying, and that the place where I'd been struck must be discolored. Whenever we encountered each other before, he'd quickly averted his eyes, as if contact with me was uncomfortable. Not that afternoon. He stared rudely as we went up the stairs to the door. I was about to reach for the handle when he stepped ahead and pulled the door open with a flourish. "After you!" he beamed. I mumbled my thanks and went in.

I thought no more of Lafont that day, but now I know it was an interesting time for him. He would have wondered about my swollen eyes, the bandage, and because he was a simple man without many points of reference, I expect he concluded that my lover had hit me in a quarrel. He may even have approved the gesture in the abstract, since he was forced to do the same with Adrienne from time to time. As for our progress up the stairs, I have no doubt that he recognized Monika's figure in mine. He could detect the movement of my buttocks even though I wore a winter coat, and his pace quickened so he would have a closer look. I turned around at the second landing because I knew what he was doing, and when I glared at him angrily he went up the next flight without a word, dismissing my indignation as his thought quickly returned to the fate of his letter. He wondered if the Germans would come when he was home, if he might hear them.

Adrienne was excited when he came in.

"The Boches were here this afternoon. They took away the woman in Number twelve."

He looked at her as casually as possible, the way the boss looked at Marie sometimes. Then he poured a glass of wine and raised it to his lips.

"Well, they didn't keep her. I just followed her upstairs."

○

"What do you think she's done?"

He shrugged as if it were too unimportant to consider.

"Who knows? He drank the wine with a flourish.

●

Monika normally finished work at four o'clock, but the baker had fallen behind and asked her to stay so that she did not leave until five-thirty, half an hour after Lafont and I went upstairs. Since Claude and Joaquín were not due home until early the next morning, she was looking forward to an evening with just the two of us. She had planned it out in advance because she decided that she was going to ask about what was happening between me and Joaquín. It was clear that we had thrived during our long days together, and she thought this would be the perfect opportunity to tell me how happy she was. She envisioned our eating dinner on the sofa together, the way we sometimes did when she was young. Although she loved Claude, and felt close to Joaquín, it was not always easy having two men in the apartment, especially when she wanted an intimate talk with her mother. And so she headed home through the snow, happy and filled with anticipation. She wanted to know how I felt, how far things had gone. She wanted to talk about America.

There were no lights in the windows of our apartment as she turned into the Rue de Seine. Her first thought was that I had gone out on an errand, or to see Madeleine, but then she remembered I hadn't mentioned leaving and she decided that I was reading in my room. As she entered the foyer Madame Morain opened her door an inch or two to see who was there. Then she came out and Monika knew something was wrong as she touched her shoulder.

"Thank God you're back! The Boches had your mother all afternoon. They took her away and she only came back an hour ago. You'd better go up right away. She's fine, I think, but you never know."

The news was so unexpected that Monika did not know what to think. The old woman was a terrible gossip, and sometimes she invented things that were wildly off the track.

"You're sure, madame?"

"I'm old, child, but I'm not blind. Now hurry!"

She went upstairs, still uncertain that Madame Morain had understood what happened. Only when she fit her key to the door and found it was unlocked did she begin to worry. I always locked the door. She could not remember an exception as she pushed it open with her foot. There was not even a sliver of light beneath my bedroom door and that was when she called to me in a frightened, childlike voice.

I had recognized her footsteps on the landing, and knew that she was frightened, but I could not answer. It was not a matter of cruelty, or inattention. I was simply exhausted. I had sat in the dark for over an hour trying to regain my sense of self, reestablish at least a portion of the identity that had been ripped from me during Munch's questioning, but I failed. I seemed to have no power to look at myself, to hover there in the darkness above the person called Ursula Krieger. I bore so little resemblance to the woman I had been earlier in the day that I thought I was dreaming and had mistaken myself for a stranger. I had tried to think of what I would do when Monika returned, when Claude and Joaquín came back from Marseilles. I could tell them what happened when the Nazis came. Tell them they had turned up no trace of Joaquín's work, that I had been taken to Munch's office. But there was no way in the world I could confess to the real source of my pain.

For that hour my quandary had been attended by the Men in the Clock who strutted and preened like peacocks. "It was stupid to think you could leave us, Ursula," one said. "Look at us. Acknowledge our presence. Give in."

The lightless room could not hide them. They were even there when I closed my eyes, visible behind that double darkness. I did not know how to make them leave. That was what I had been thinking of when she called again. They were all around me and I had to answer. "Don't worry," I said. "I'm fine."

She switched on the light. It was a little miracle, because my visitors fled in a flutter of arms and mechanical sounds. They flew off, frightened by the light, and all that was left of them was the ticking of the clock on the table beside me.

She knelt down and took my hand.

"Madame Morain told me."

"I'm fine," I said, shielding my eyes with my hand.

"Then it's true?"

"Yes, but they know nothing about Joaquín. That's what is important."

Then I knew I was safe. I should have realized all along that the story of the Nazis would explain my condition. I hadn't thought of it because I was so busy fending off my visitors. So I told her everything, except my conversation with Munch. I felt better, stronger as I talked, but I had no idea how I looked.

Much later, while we were waiting through the interminable delay in Lisbon, we talked about that night. She told me that she'd had two shocks. The first was the news from Madame Morain. The second and strongest, because she did not understand it, was a memory. As she knelt beside me she recalled a moment in childhood with extraordinary clarity. She had seen that expression in my mirror early one morning when she could not sleep and had gone into my room just as I was beginning to comb my hair. I combed carefully, slowly, very deliberately, and it had been interesting to her, seeing me lavish that kind of attention on my hair. At first she could only see the back of my head, the strands of my hair gleaming in the lamplight. But then she came a little closer and was about to speak when she saw my face in the mirror. She said I had looked so far away, so unlike myself, that she returned to her room and lay in bed for a long time trying to understand why she could not say anything.

"Do you remember, Mother? Was that a special night of some kind? Had something happened?"

I thought how pleased my visitors would be to hear those questions. I said, "Do you remember that expression any other time?" If she said yes I would have been truly devastated. She had not. I looked at her and said, "Well, then, it was probably nothing. You know how I am sometimes."

I did not go to the station with her the next morning. Joaquín told me later that he knew something had happened when he saw her pushing through the crowd, and he was not surprised when she told them about the informer and Munch's appearance. He had not been able to rid himself of the feeling that came upon him at the Château d'If. All the way back he felt off balance, oppressed. But it was me he had worried about. It never occurred to him that he also fit into the equation.

Monika had been relieved to see them, but after she explained what happened she seemed distant and almost angry. It didn't take long to realize that she resented him, blamed him for my ordeal. He told Claude that we had to leave. The tickets for the ship could not be moved up for an earlier departure, but nothing was keeping us in Paris except a few things Claude could take care of quickly. The important thing was getting out. He was convinced that we were both in danger, and I could not make him understand that Munch didn't care about me.

We might have argued longer than we did if he hadn't removed two squares of tissue paper from his pocket and given them to Monika and me. Inside were identical sets of silver earrings, each strung with a single blue trader's bead. I put mine on, and have worn them every day.

Since none of us could be certain that Munch and his men might not return, Joaquín insisted on going to stay with St. Omer. He planned to come back Friday morning, when we would go together to the station. With Joaquín safe in the suburbs I could once again believe in the dream of freedom we had made for ourselves. Of course I knew that the unexpected might rear its head at any moment, but it seemed unlikely now. Having a firm date, knowing the time our train would leave, restored my confidence, and I was able to see Munch's appearance at the door the day before almost as a good omen.

There was much to do. Leaving home with only what one can carry requires careful consideration. Claude had to make arrangements for his classes, and Monika insisted on going to see her teacher. She owed Madame Lemonnier an unrepayable debt, and wanted to spend the day with her.

Claude and Monika left after breakfast. Joaquín had contacted St. Omer and intended to leave with them, but I asked him to stay awhile. The chance of another visit from the Nazis that morning was remote, and there were things I had to say, things I had thought about since I'd tried to pass off the effects of my afternoon at Gestapo headquarters.

Odd as it sounds, I had discovered that I was grateful to Munch for his barbarous behavior. As I walked home through the snow, humiliated and filled with guilt, I was appalled by how quickly my past had been brought to light. I had lived with it, endured it for over fifteen years, made accommodations, accepted the visitations of the Men in the Clock. Even when the news came about Claude's position, and I could think of a new life away from Paris, I had been able to convince myself that I could go on carrying my secret with me, that it would not affect whatever life Joaquín and I would make for ourselves in America.

But Munch had shown a light into the deeper recesses of my mind. It was not appreciably different from what happened before when my visitors came, but this light was brighter and revealed a truth I had hidden because I could not accept it. I could continue deceiving Joaquín. He would never know. My expertise in masking the causes of my depressions after my friends appeared was the equal of any artist's who stands before a canvas and knows, without having to think about it, what must be done, how the space should be divided, what colors the forms would take. If the war had suddenly ended and we had been free to return to our old lives, I know I would not have found the courage to reach down and bring my life at the Seven Dolphins up into the light. But it was not ending. We were only a few days away from going into exile, and I was still a crippled refugee from Old Berlin.

So I asked Joaquín to stay awhile, willing to face the risk that Munch might descend once more, even willing to jeopardize his safety in order that I might bind my days together. Only then could we leave as two whole beings, the past no longer shadowed with deceit.

It was freezing cold. I made a pot of ersatz coffee, which we drank in the living room. He had placed the things he would take to Jacques's on the table, along with the manuscript of the *Letters*. He wanted to write about Munch and Valdés. If it turned out well, he would arrange for it to be published the following week. It seemed appropriate for the last of the *Letters* he would write in France to focus on them, and he spoke intently about what he proposed to do.

I listened carefully, but at the same time I was trying to decide how to begin. What I had to say filled me like a pregnancy that had taken years to come to term. I was frightened, aware of doubts, not as to the wisdom of my decision, but whether I could find the words to say exactly what needed to be said. Yes, I was aware that I might lose him. Even though I believed in his compassion, there was the risk that I would touch some place in his heart I had not seen, open an old wound, stir a latent fear over which he had no more control than I did when my visitors came. But I could no more stop what was on the way than I could have prohibited Monika coming into the world once the labor pains took hold and wrenched my innermost being. I could not stop what was coming, and there was a certain comfort in that knowledge. If what I said did not kill his feeling for me, we would leave France in four days' time. It seemed to me that our new life, his and mine, Claude's and Monika's, was already visible over the horizon, that once again the shape of my desire was as clear as the sun rising from the morning sea.

What happened then I did not foresee. He had finished talking about the *Letters* and was trying to explain his premonition at the Château d'If. When he'd understood I was in jeopardy a sudden weakness had taken hold of him, as if he were ill. "I wanted to help you, but there was nothing I could do. It was like a dream." I looked at him, and it was as if all the fear left me in that instant. I wanted him near me so that our embrace could answer the apprehension he still so clearly felt. I wanted one last time together in the event that what I said would make it the last. So I rose and went to him, held his face, kissed him. "It's cold out here," I said.

We were used to each other by then, knew instinctively how to please, what response to expect or exact, though this time I brought different expectations to our lovemaking. I was neither more nor less passionate than before, neither hurried nor languorous, but there was something elegiac in my love, as if my body were preparing my heart and mind for what might follow.

Afterward I sat up and leaned against the bed frame, pulling the blankets up for warmth. I took his hand, folding my fingers into his. "Please remember that is who we are."

He looked questioningly at me, as if I had made a joke. Then he saw how serious I was.

"Of course," he said. "But why?"

"I'll tell you in a minute. First you must promise to remember, because I am going to tell you something you will not want to hear. It will hurt, but I have no choice—you must understand that, Joaquín. Afterward you can decide if it changes anything between us. It may, but I can't hide it any longer. We can't be together unless I do."

"Nothing is that important, Ursula."

"Yes, something is."

His eyes changed then. It was so subtle that anyone who did

181

not know him well would have missed it, but I saw it the way I see the water darken under clouds.

"It's why you sent me away."

I nodded, adding, "I couldn't talk about it then. Now I have to. You remember when I told you about the white dolphins? There were others, not white but gray, who swam in a sign above a certain street."

The story came sluggishly, slowly, haltingly, as if it had to struggle from my throat along the corrugated surface of an unwilling tongue, prying my teeth open, then my lips. At first I felt short of breath, and that must have accounted for the flatness of my tone, which sounded affectless as that of persons suffering some irremediable damage to their emotions. My voice was like a record played on a Victrola I had not wound tight, but the low, dolorous sound soon gained in speed and intensity, and finally the pitch was one I recognized as mine. Just before it came Joaquín reached over and touched my lips, as if to say I need not go on, but I shook my head, said, "No, it's the only way." A moment later I took him with me to Old Berlin, holding his hand as if I were walking through those remembered streets, afraid that any moment now he would rise and leave. I knew that my stoicism, my almost casual statement that he was free to decide, had been mere bravado. I would hold on to him as long as I was able.

As soon as I explained the nature of the Seven Dolphins I felt myself relax, tension giving way to frankness buoyed up with relief. I told him everything, saw everything as I had remembered it over the years. There were times when I was surprised by what I'd made of certain scenes and persons. Above all, I saw how I had transformed the Men in the Clock into figures who scarcely resembled their originals, who now were only men, some good, some corrupt, who had come to slake their lust with me and other women. As I described them I heard their voices as they had come to me, sly, insinuating voices that threatened or cajoled, and it seemed they were becoming fainter as I continued, that their power of speech had been gained by my silence and secrecy.

I remember them all. I told him how, in a vain effort to distance myself, I gave them numbers for names, reinventing them in the shapes of figures in clock towers. But I did not talk about One, or Two, or Seven or Eight or Nine because that would have been to capitulate to a weakness I no longer felt. No, I restored their names, not even surprised that I could remember after all those years. The numbers had been both veils and mnemonic devices, and I could not finally forget them until I spoke them all aloud.

I remembered Klaus Schloezer, known throughout the Seven Dolphins as The Weeper, who came to all of us like an animal in heat, fervent and urgent in his desires which, when slaked, left him with tears in his eyes and a whimper in his voice as he begged me never to tell his mother what he had done.

I remembered Eric Sturmer, the rotund banker, who always wanted me to say I loved him—loved his fat, hairless stomach—and who promised to pay double for those words. When I would not he paid anyway, saying that once I knew him better I would see what a splendid fellow he was.

I remembered Dieter, a boy of about seventeen, who was always amazed that he was in bed with a woman, and who never seemed to understand that any of us were more than a vessel for his incontinent desires.

I remembered more than I named, and as I told Joaquín, opened my past to him, I heard doors slamming, windows closing, saw the Men in the Clock falling from their high estate, which my guilt and anguish had granted them. I wept because I knew it was final, that they would never come again, wept because I had had to wait so long to name them and knew that that, all along, had been the key to my release.

Joaquín did not flinch. I asked him about it afterward because it seemed impossible that somewhere in his mind he would not have felt appalled. He did not. He said that even before I began he knew, though why or how was a mystery to him. The best he could do was connect it with his premonition at the Château d'If, and then to Munch.

I listened as carefully as I ever had to another human being, waiting for some word or gesture that would reveal a breach between us, but none appeared. Instead, he said something that convinced me we had passed the danger I feared would be the end of us.

"I never understood what the white dolphins were until just now. And I wonder if you did, Ursula."

I had no idea what would follow, and I must say I did not care. Sometimes he talked dreamily about things that caught his fancy, and it seemed that he was headed in that direction when he said, "I accepted them as figures in a dream. Now I see what they really were, your magic. They came like creatures in folk tales and allowed you to escape."

That was the only thing he ever said about my story. Afterward it was as if I had never spoken to him that morning, but I knew he was not ignoring what I said. It was simply past, and his understanding of that time in my life was bound to those svelte white creatures who bore me away from all I could not bear.

I wished there were some way we could spend the day together, but it was already close to noon, and Joaquín insisted that he had to leave to meet St. Omer. After he left I waited by the window until I saw him through the frost-rimmed glass as he went along the street and disappeared. The frost was pale blue, and I thought of the rolling plains in southern France, the shadows of the Pyrénées where they came down to the sea, then of this very sea I now travel on. In a few days I would see it. Already there was a freshening of the apartment's stale air, a scent of seaweed and salt and the distant sound of gulls calling on the wind.

12

Joaquín and Jacques spent that Sunday afternoon going over the plans we'd made for our departure. They were both in a foul mood because it was very likely they would not see each other again. Neither mentioned it until they finished dinner when Jacques said gruffly that he would miss him. "The war is temporary, Wolf, but exile tends to become a permanent condition." "Then come to America," Joaquín said. "Visit me in Pacific Palisades." "You know me better than that, Wolf. I'm too old to travel now. We will have to become epic correspondents."

After dinner Elizabeth left them alone with a bottle of calvados, and they talked about their work until it was gone. When Jacques held the empty bottle up and asked if he should open another, Joaquín said that he had had enough. Besides being tired, Jacques was in one of his moods, and Joaquín knew it would only get worse if they drank more.

Although they were old friends, they had rarely talked about what brought them together. Like most men, they would have been embarrassed by any overt display of emotion, but things had changed. Since leaving me at noon, Joaquín had thought about what I had told him off and on during the day. He was deeply moved, and the knowledge that he and Jacques had only a few days left broke down what was left of his reserve. He thanked him again for giving him a place to stay.

"Idiot! What do you think I'd say?"

They looked at each other without knowing what to do. Finally Joaquín said, "I'll miss you."

They embraced. Jacques stood back a moment later, his hands on Joaquín's shoulders. "Be careful, Wolf. I won't feel good about this until I have a letter from California."

That was how their day ended, with a long-delayed and unavoidably melancholy acknowledgment of friendship. Exhausted by my confession and the pain of leaving St. Omer, Joaquín fell into bed and was instantly asleep.

I had spent the day alone thinking about the change that had come upon me. Already it seemed that we were different people than we had been that morning. I do not mean that I was obsessed by our conversation, only that I perceived the day through the peace it brought me. I didn't know what to expect, probably a rush of thoughts, misgivings, forgotten opportunities to emphasize something here, alter something there. But I suffered none of that. I was too relieved, too tired to replay it all. It must be that way with everyone after such a purging. And so I napped, I thought of Monika and Madame Lemonnier, of Claude meeting with his colleagues and afterward in his office, trying to decide what to take to America.

By noon dark clouds threatened snow, and the Rue de Seine was deserted. I remember looking at the abandoned street with a feeling of gratitude. At the time I was happy to be alone, but I wonder now what might have happened if I'd grown restless and decided to go for a walk. This is not idle speculation. Everyone can point to a handful of days when something momentous happened to change their lives—a birth, a death, a sudden rise or fall in fortune. My confession and Joaquín's response certainly qualified, but there was more. I have been forced to think about that day many times, and always it seems to me that if I had left the apartment and gone, say, as far as the stairs of the Basilica of Sacré-Coeur, I might have had some intimation of the changes that would soon come upon us. Since I stayed inside, I have no other choice than to recreate and expand upon what I learned later from St. Omer and stories in the papers. Though there are facts to guide me now, they are incomplete, and I must rely once again, as I did with Guy Lafont, on my imagination. What I see is vivid and precise, the way it would have been if I had looked down from the heights of Montmartre and seen two young Nazi soldiers buttoning their greatcoats as they left their quarters and went along the icy streets to Mass at Notre Dame.

I think of them as simple country boys, both religious without ever having thought deeply about such matters, and I expect each was grateful to have found someone else who shared his beliefs. They would have been uncomfortable in Paris because it was impossibly different than the little farming towns they came from, and whenever they were together they would have cheered each other up with stories about home and family.

These boys, Josef and Otto, believed in the Reich, though both were secretly relieved they had not seen combat. When they talked about the possibility of being sent to the front, each insisted that he was willing to kill for the Fatherland, though neither mentioned anything about dying *pro patria*. In their hearts they were afraid of death. For Josef, it was always the image of his grandfather lying in his coffin. For Otto, it was a mask he had seen during a Walpurgisnacht celebration when he was ten.

That morning their thoughts were far from death. The priest had absolved them of their sins. Josef confessed to a yearning to visit a brothel, Otto to impure thoughts about a shopgirl which he had satisfied with solitary love. After they spoke of their desires in the dark confessionals they listened, chastened and grateful for their penances, as another priest intoned the Mass, his Latin syllables filling the cathedral with spiritual comfort and promised ease.

The clouds had blown away to the east by the time Mass was over. Neither felt like returning to the garrison and they decided, on the spur of the moment, to walk as far as the Luxembourg Gardens and then find a good café for lunch. They were used to spending long days outside in winter, and both felt a youthful superiority to the people who seemed bent on going home as fast as possible. Since it was too cold to walk on the shady side of the street, they crossed into the sun at the Boulevard St. Germain. Had it been summer, they would have chosen a bench and chatted until they felt hungry, but the park was even colder than the streets had been. Besides, the denuded trees were stark and melancholy, and so they agreed to walk through as quickly as possible and have an early lunch.

They saw Munch just as they reached the far side of the park. Josef was enormously surprised, for the Obersturmführer appeared to be sitting behind a scrawny bush at the base of a skeletal tree. He glanced at Otto, pointed, and they went forward, afraid now, and glad for each other's company.

Munch was, in fact, leaning against the trunk of a plane tree and as they approached, Josef nudged Otto's arm. "He's probably just drunk." "No," Otto whispered, "Look."

Munch's naked legs showed like two large fish against the snow. His pants and underwear were piled beside him. His visored SS hat lay almost jauntily in his lap. At that distance he might have been yawning, but as they drew closer they saw that his mouth was propped open with a twig wedged between his upper and lower teeth. Later, Josef told the soldiers in his garrison that the mouth appeared fixed in an eternal scream, but it would have been a silent scream because someone had cut out his tongue.

As soon as Otto understood what he was looking at he fell to his knees and became violently ill, moaning and vomiting while Josef stared, unable to believe what he saw. The only reference point for such a thing in his experience was nightmares and, as in a nightmare, he had no power to move. He knew he should run to the nearest building and telephone his superiors, but he also knew that Munch was beyond the need for help. And so, after reaching down and patting Otto's shoulder, a gesture which only increased his moans, Josef approached the nightmare.

Munch's legs were splayed out like the fork of a tree. His polished boots shone brightly, even in the mottled sunlight. Josef did not look into the gaping, tongueless mouth. All his attention was on the hat resting between Munch's legs. He reached down slowly, as in a dream, afraid of what he was going to see, but powerless to stop his fingers closing on the arched peak of the hat. He did not look until he had straightened up.

Josef was convinced that Munch had been castrated, or that his penis had been cut off. He almost sighed with relief when he saw the intact genitals looking as normal as his own, except that they were pulled to the side by a piece of coarse string lashed to Munch's thigh. When he saw what they had done he joined Otto on the snow, falling away from the dead officer onto his hands and knees. He closed his eyes as the sickness erupted, but the image was indelibly impressed upon his mind. The cleft between Munch's buttocks loomed large as a cave. The gelatinous piece of flesh had been inserted into his anus, and the tip protruded in a bloody parody of a child sticking out his tongue.

●

St. Omer read the Resistance papers as well as those co-opted by the Nazis. "It amuses me to see how many lies the swine can think of," he said once. It was his habit to go out at noon to a newsstand not far from his house, and that was what he did the next day. He returned twenty minutes later muttering to himself.

"Read that," he said, handing Joaquín the paper. "Then we'll have to talk about what to do."

The story of Munch's death was splashed across the front page. There was no doubt that the Resistance was responsible, and the High Command had issued an order that ten hostages would be shot in reprisal.

During the last year there had been numerous killings. Most of the time the Nazis' names were not mentioned. But Munch had been highly visible, and when Joaquín saw his name he was happy. He had been outraged by what Munch had done to me, hated him for the humiliation. He tried to conjure up an image of him from what I had said, but Munch remained a faceless cipher in his imagination, and somehow that increased his anger. At the same time, violence such as had been perpetrated on Gerhard Munch lay beyond his understanding, and he actually experienced revulsion, even a sense of guilt, after his first reaction. It would have taken more than Nazis to brutalize him, and that is another reason why I loved him.

As soon as he put the paper down St. Omer picked it up, balled the sheet, and tossed it into the coal bin. "This is the one who took Ursula?"

"There's no question."

"Well then, Wolf, I think you will have to leave immediately. They can't ignore this, not with someone of his stature. They'll look high and low. It stands to reason they'll check on his recent investigations."

St. Omer was right, of course, and Joaquín cursed himself for coming to stay with us. We were all in danger because of him.

"Listen," St. Omer said. "I'll go now and tell them."

"No. It's my responsibility."

"Damn it, Wolf, they're probably looking for you. It's obvious the informer gave them a description. That scar of yours doesn't help. Now let's work this out. I'll do the leg work."

St. Omer arrived two hours later, prepared to tell us what had happened, but we too had seen the papers. Joaquín would stay with him that night. On Tuesday morning, as soon as the curfew was lifted, they would come to get us and we would go to the Gare d'Austerlitz. The idea was that we would appear more like a family if there were five of us.

Claude, Monika and I spent the rest of the day packing. It was one of the longest days of my life. Doubt about what might happen hung in the frigid air. It seemed to me that I could reach out and touch it, and it only became worse after dark. From time to time we looked out at the street, expecting to see men watching the apartment. There were none, but that was not encouraging because they could come at any moment. There was no certainty about our plan, no certainty about anything. We went to bed after midnight, but I slept only fitfully, and whenever I did I returned to the same dream. I saw Munch in the park, rejoiced at his death and mutilation. Then, to my horror, he slowly stood up, his tongueless mouth moving in frustration that he could not shout my name as he stumbled toward me, pointing, his eyes wild with hatred.

That dream was all I remembered of the night before we left. Since then its darkness has been filled out, its terrain peopled with a fuller picture of what followed in the wake of Munch's death. Our neighbors never impinged on my thoughts. For all I knew, there was nothing above our ceiling but the frigid night air, a moonless sky. But now I know there was something else. Oh yes, I have had time to understand what was above me. The thought is as insistent as a toothache, a pain in the gut, a fever that lies unabated on one's brow.

Lafont was pacing back and forth, racking his brains to understand his inexplicable fall from grace. He had started drink-

191

ing as soon as he read about Munch. When Adrienne saw what he was up to she demanded an explanation, but he ignored her and filled his glass to the brim. Already a little tipsy, he had managed to construe Munch's death as a personal loss of honor, and he sat at the scarred table as if he were the only patron in a bar, listening to Adrienne cleaning up, watching her blow on her fingers to warm them. At that moment she was no more to him than a nameless barmaid who made him feel even more alone. He remembered what it was like with Vautrin only a few days ago at La Belle Reine, how confident and proud he felt. Then the humiliation set in. Vautrin would have told the others about his generosity, the way he handled himself. They would be expecting something soon. In a few weeks, a month at most, they would know. He could not bear the thought of his impending humiliation.

Much later, when he fell into bed, lurid dreams troubled his sleep. He was alternately living in an elegant hotel on the Right Bank, then in an apartment much poorer than where he slept. Once all the fellows at work treated him like royalty, then they were laughing, pointing at him, calling him names. He wanted to run away, but they were closing in on him, accusing him of lying, of being too big for himself.

He woke at five o'clock in a sweat with a terrible headache. He prodded Adrienne in the ribs.

"Get me some aspirin. A glass of wine."

He swallowed the pills and drank off the wine even though it tasted vile. He knew from experience that was the only way to treat such a head. He went down the hall to piss. Emptying his bladder made him feel better, but now he was fully awake. As soon as he remembered why he had gotten drunk, he launched into an invective against Munch for getting himself killed. He was positive the Germans had found out something about his mysterious neighbor, equally certain that Munch planned to present a munificent reward, perhaps even call on him to be his eyes and ears in the neighborhood. Such things happened all the time. The loss was so painful that he poured another drink, confident that he would sober up in time for work.

He was standing in the kitchen. It had begun to snow and when he went over to the window to watch he saw Monika standing on the sidewalk. It occurred to him that she must be on the way to work. He imagined her breasts moving rhythmically as she kneaded dough. The fantasy was developing nicely until the rest of us joined her and he realized we were leaving. When Joaquín and St. Omer started down the street Lafont banged on the window. "Stop!" he shouted. Adrienne sat bolt upright in bed as he hurried to the door and went downstairs, cursing all the way. When he passed Madame Morain's door he heard her call "What is it? Who's there?" but he ignored her, flung open the door and ran toward us shouting, "Traitor! I know who you are!" He stopped only when Joaquín turned to see who it was. "Come on, now!" St. Omer said, quickening his pace, but I had to look at the man who was so obviously drunk, still wearing his pajamas and shivering from cold and anger.

"Ursula!" Joaquín hissed. "Let's go!"

I couldn't. Suddenly I knew this was the rat in the attic but I could not believe it. I don't know what I thought he'd look like. Perhaps tall and thin, with a wandering eye. Old and sour. A cursing, epicene dandy. It should have been anyone but this squat man whose hairy belly protruded through his unbuttoned pajama top. But it was Lafont who brought Munch to life and forced us to leave. I hated him. I pitied him. Emotion broke over me in a wave of bitter laughter. It seemed impossibly comical that it was this man whose eyes had burned into my buttocks whenever I went up the stairs. He was as absurd as my memory of Old Berlin. "Sweet Christ, Joaquín, he's the one," I said as I hurried along beside him. "You came within a hair's breadth of being discovered because of him."

I looked back over my shoulder just as Lafont shouted "Stop!" one more time. He watched us disappear around the corner, and I expect he stood there for another minute ignoring the cold as he wondered what to do, but his mind had gone blank. The only thing he knew was that his reward had vanished in the snow.

When he returned to his apartment he took off his soaked pajamas and pulled a drawer from the chest so far out that it clattered onto the floor, but he did not care. He quickly put on a dry pair of pajamas and then his robe. He was shivering as he went to the cabinet for the cognac. Adrienne lay in bed, crying. "I don't understand," she said. "What's the matter?" And then, when she saw him with the bottle, her patience snapped. "Don't! You'll never be able to work. They'll fire you, and then where will we be?"

He glanced malevolently at her. The curlers in her hair bulged under a faded bandanna. He wanted her to be Monika.

"Shut up. I do as I please."

He drank the cognac and poured another, after which he sat down at the kitchen table with his back to the window, to the traitorous snow. Our departure proved he was right. He'd suspected Joaquín all along, he was no one's fool, and he deserved something for his perspicacity, some recognition. Munch was dead, but there were other Gestapo. He could tell them how we had sneaked away minutes after the curfew was lifted.

He did not go any further with his thinking that morning. An hour later Adrienne helped him stagger into bed where, before he passed out, he muttered something about deserving to be paid. "For what?" she asked sarcastically. "What do you deserve?"

He slept like a dead man until a little past three in the afternoon when Adrienne's shrill voice, accompanied, it seemed, by other voices, men's voices, penetrated his drunkenness. He rolled over and told her to shut up, and she shook him violently. "Leave me alone!" he muttered as he flailed at her with his hand. She struck him on the ear and he sat up with a terrible ringing in his head to see a soldier standing over him with his hand balled into a fist, ready to hit him again.

I imagine that since Munch's death, Nazi patrols had been out in force, questioning anyone whose name appeared in his files. Lafont, along with the others, was taken to the Rue des Saussaies where three men interrogated him about his letter, insinuating that he was a member of the Resistance. He wanted to cry because of the pain from his hangover and the pain in his ear. His hearing was affected, and he pleaded for a doctor. Later, they said. First the truth.

He said he supported the Vichy government. He described how Joaquín and the rest of us escaped at dawn, but they laughed at his story.

"It proves nothing," one of them said.

Lafont crossed himself. "As God is my witness, I saw them go. They were all Resistance. They killed Munch, I know it."

The Nazis neither believed nor disbelieved. Sometimes the truth took a little time, a little persuasion, and they were prepared to wait. They had no doubt they would discover Lafont's truth, and they were determined to make an example of everyone in their search for Munch's assassin. So he was locked up with many others, and it was then that what little luck remaining to him was lost.

An administrative blunder caused him to be housed with a group of detainees destined for the labor camps. All the while protesting his innocence, he could not believe how fate had tricked him. He was shuttled from one holding cell to another, given bowls of disgusting gruel once a day, and finally trucked to a railway station with dozens of men and women and children. As they were herded into wooden cars he protested his innocence only to be struck on the head with a rifle butt. His injured ear ached, rang, went dead. The voices in the car, the whispers, cries, and moans, the steady clicking of the wheels, entered his good ear only, contributing to his misery and increasing his rage as he asked and asked where he was being taken. Finally he too fell silent, drifting off into a fitful half sleep only to be awakened by the harsh rumbling of the doors sliding open. As he stepped onto the platform he was blinded by floodlights.

No one ever heard of Lafont again. I imagine only an immense darkness through which he fell, screaming, protesting his innocence, his voice lost in the cries of others as the doors of the huge room closed behind them.

That terrible recognition of Lafont's end came to me only just now. At the time we hurried down the street, he was still merely the rat in the attic, though his hateful features stayed with me until we boarded the métro. Then, out of necessity, and because what I had hoped for was beginning to happen, I forgot him and looked ahead.

It was snowing hard when we came out of the Austerlitz stop. Two or three inches had accumulated in the streets, and by the time we reached the station we were covered with fine powder. The stark roof arching overhead seemed to condense the cold. People pulled their coats tight, blew on red fingers, children cried, but it made no difference. As we made our way to the platform where our train waited, the lights in its cars shone as brightly as decorations on Christmas trees, glistening with more promise than I thought possible because we had shaken off more than snow when we entered the station. We had also left a large part of our fear and apprehension on the dirty pavement where it was dissolving even then, forming harmless puddles through which people walked carelessly, obliterating it even as we reached our car. We were not safe yet, not completely out of danger, but soon we would be.

St. Omer's eyes were red and he daubed impatiently at them, disdainfully wiping away the tears. The show of emotion embarrassed him. I realized it would be easier for him and Joaquín to say goodbye if we boarded, so I took Claude and Monika by the arm and pushed them ahead of me up the stairs. Joaquín did not follow until the conductor's shrill whistle sounded beneath the iron girders of the arching roof.

For what must have been the tenth time that morning we

checked our passports and visas. Then we went over our plan, questioning, explaining, clarifying, confident that nothing had been overlooked. We knew what to expect at the border. A friend of Joaquín's at the Lorca Club knew Port Bou and the surrounding countryside from having grown up in Gerona. Weeks ago he had drawn a detailed map of the area, as well as a diagram of the station. We had each memorized every detail, knew all the relevant distances, the lay of the land along the Costa Brava. If need be, we knew how to circumvent the station and pass through the adjoining fields to the path that would take us through the mountains into Spain. Night after night we had asked "What if?" and then put our heads together until we discovered solutions to the most unlikely contingencies. We became scholars of the border, our minds a collective archive of Port Bou. And we went into our archive once more as we waited for the first tug of the engine, the clatter of couplings that would send us on our way. Already I saw the tracks snaking through the countryside, aware that every kilometer we put between ourselves and Paris would strengthen me, allow me to breathe more freely. Already I smelled the salt air, which was more pungent than when I'd imagined it weeks ago, saw the sun on the water of Lisbon harbor, watched burly sailors casting off the lines.

Joaquín sat next to me in the window seat, Claude and Monika facing us. They smiled when the car suddenly inched forward. St. Omer appeared in the window, made a sign with his thumb extended, and then he fell behind with the platform.

"I'll miss him," Joaquín said.

"We all will," Claude answered. "Maybe he'll come to America some day."

Joaquín had been wound up tight since I'd first seen him earlier that morning. Now I felt him relax, and when I looked his eyes were closed. His beard gave him a patriarchal, almost a rabbinical appearance, and I approved of the disguise. The clean-shaven man I'd met was gone. He removed the black-rimmed glasses and I put them in my bag.

Monika was talking to Claude about Madame Lemonnier's parting gift, her favorite camera, a Rolleiflex. She was happy explaining its functions to Claude, and their energy made me feel old. I glanced at Joaquín, a little surprised that he could leave Paris for the last time without watching it slip by, but there was really very little to see because of the gusting snow. Besides, the whole city was in his head. I wondered if I should rest too. There was nothing to interest me in the dreary brick buildings running alongside the track. There had been such anxiety, such a frenzy of worry and preparation, but I was not willing to give in to my fatigue until we passed into the countryside. The snow gusted, sometimes blotting out everything, sometimes opening up so that I could see a cornice, a chimney, plane trees. The city was ordered now by the regular clicking of the wheels, the pleasant rocking of the car. It was opening up beyond the veil of snow, parting like an unseen gate, then closing behind us, sealing off Lafont, Munch, the Men in the Clock. Most of all it was closing on the old Ursula. I remembered the train Monika and I had taken away from Berlin and how I had drawn the curtains. They were open now, and I looked ahead, in the direction of my desire.

And what of Joaquín? It is not hard to imagine. He must have been thinking how far he had come since the days when he rose before dawn and went into the streets in search of the city's first sounds as it stretched and came awake. He would have thought, too, of how he had lived inside Heinz's mind, seen through his eyes, and how all of that was buried now in the cardboard matchbox. He would have grieved for Paris, but he would have changed nothing because he had the *Letters* and he was going to America. He had heard that a road ran the length of the coast of California, and he wanted us to see that coast, to hire a car and drive south from San Francisco. He had a splendid vision of green cliffs breaking away to sand beaches, sailboats. He would publish the *Letters* in America and eventually in Spain, where they truly belonged.

And he would have thought about Lorca. Of that I have no doubt. Never in all the time that had passed since their meeting had he forgotten Granada, the city of fountains, of trellises dripping jasmine, of the stone fantasies of the Alhambra. He still mourned the fact that Lorca had loved it because it was also the city of the Falange and the power of the priests, a place where the dead mind of the Inquisition flowered in the mind of Luis Valdés.

I remember him looking out at the white fields, and then, quite suddenly, he recited the "Romance Sonámbulo."

> *The night grew intimate*
> *like a little square.*
> *Drunken Civil Guards*
> *were beating on the door.*
> *Green, I want you green.*
> *Green wind. Green boughs.*
> *The ship on the sea.*
> *And the horse in the mountains.*

He told me that those lines had led him to the conclusion of his last *Letter*, and I thought of it as the train went south.

Where is Lorca? Look around the stand of olive trees, beyond the pool of Ainadamar. There is nothing to see, not on the surface. They put him in the ground with no marker, buried him with the one-legged schoolmaster and the singer of flamenco. But look in your mind. You will find him there. They will try to invade your mind, make it smooth as the pale ground of Fuente Grande. They will try to cover what is in your mind as they tried to cover what happened there with sapling pines. But Lorca defies them. He is there in the pines, the green wind, the green boughs. That is where he is in your minds, if you only look, where the trees have grown beyond the reach of those who planted them.

199

Beyond Toulouse there was no more snow, only mist the color of gray watercolor, which reduced the farmlands to abstract fields marked here and there by stone walls or tottering fences. Joaquín turned up his collar against the cold as he waited for Carcassonne. He was afraid that the mist would hang over the land and obscure the view, but it lifted before we reached the plain and the ancient city came into view several kilometers east of the tracks. The distance should have diminished it, but that was not the case. It rose from the rolling hills and its peaked towers, its barbicans, every detail he could make out was even better than he remembered. This was the last image he wanted of France, and he sat forward in order to see better, resting his hands on his knees as the city drifted by, its walls red in the wan sunlight. The rhythmic clicking of the wheels seemed to change their pitch, and it took no effort at all to hear the sound of a tambourine, phrases of a troubadour's complaint.

Then it grew smaller as we passed and he pressed his face close to the window to watch the cones of the towers, which seemed black as witches' hats, and gleamed in the twilight like the patent leather of the Guardia Civil. He thought of other music then, the strong voice of a singer, hands clapping a flamenco rhythm, and that imagined music welcomed him into Spain long before he ever saw it. He wished that we could delay our departure and go to one of the coastal villages with emerald coves where white walls and red tiled roofs winked like so many colored eyes at the placid sea. He wanted to put his feet down in Spain for a while, walk on it as he remembered the stone seawall above the beach in Llfranch, the little square below the pine knoll where brass bands played on weekends, and people in gaily colored costumes danced the sardana.

"What is it?" I asked.

"I was thinking of a place on the coast where I went once, long ago. I was thinking about how it would be if we could go there and dance, just once. It is a strange and lovely music that they play."

We looked at each other when the train slowed down. Now that we had reached the border the compartment seemed very small. The tracks curved on the way into Port Bou, wound round in a gentle arc that allowed us to see the station lights in the distance. There was a shudder and the squeal of breaks. We had arrived.

Minutes later other passengers were already massing before two customs booths manned by French border police. When the Guardia Civil passed beneath the bare bulbs hanging from the corrugated iron roof their hats shone brightly, as if they had a life of their own.

We had decided weeks ago that it would be prudent to wait a while before leaving the compartment, reasoning that those at the head of the lines would be subjected to closer scrutiny. Now there appeared to be some commotion and Monika said that she was going to see what it was. That was part of our careful plan. It had seemed that because she was the least suspicious-looking of us, she could go ahead in a situation such as this and make certain that the procedures had not been altered. If they had, we would have a few minutes to decide what to do.

"Be careful," Joaquín said.

"I'll be back in five minutes."

As soon as she reached the platform I saw two Guardia Civil approach an elderly couple. They seemed to be demanding their papers, which the man quickly produced. Everyone around them looked worried. All along the line people breathed clouds of frost that were very bright beneath the lights.

Five minutes passed. Ten. "I can't stand it," I said, and got up to see about Monika. Joaquín put his hand on my arm and reminded me that we must follow our plan.

"I see her," Claude said, "just over there, talking to some people."

I saw her too, and even at that distance I could tell she was worried. Something was happening at the head of the first line. Those in the second were allowed through. I could see people closing their bags and heading up the platform on the Spanish side to the waiting trains.

Monika was anguished when she returned. The Spaniards had closed the border to everyone without French passports. She had seen some German citizens being herded into a waiting room. "They'll be sent back in the morning. There's a train coming from Barcelona."

We would have to walk over the mountains to Gerona where we could catch a train to Lisbon. Joaquín told Claude to go out and check the tracks toward the rear of the train. He would do the same on the platform side. They returned in a few minutes, neither of them having seen any guards. We would leave on the side of the car away from the platform, cross the tracks, and make our way across the fields.

The door at the end of the car opened onto a coupling covered with ice. A handrail sloped down beside the narrow steps. When we were gathered beside the car Joaquín pointed toward the rear of the train. The last car stood outside the platform's overhang, and it looked very large and menacing in the dark. We crossed the tracks quickly and soon found ourselves on the far side of the station. A single bulb in a conical fixture high on the wall sputtered, went out, came on long enough for me to see a sign in washed-out letters announcing Port Bou, España.

A full moon made the fields blue in the shadow of the mountain. We followed the path up to the first ridge, crowned with black pines, and the trees reminded me of the towers of Carcassonne. The snow was frozen hard as a crust of day-old bread, and whenever our feet broke the surface the sound seemed loud as a bowl shattering on a marble floor. As we started up the pass our breath looked like musical notes assigning duration to our steps. To the left there was fenced pasture where several horses stood close together, trying to warm themselves. The moon was growing brighter all the time, and I tried to think of nothing but the sharp edge of the ridge marking the border and the unseen coastal plain beyond. There was movement in the darkness.

"What is it?" I whispered, but the others had not seen it. We went on and then, in a space between two trees, I saw the horse and rider. There was a flash, and Joaquín fell beside me. Only as I bent down did I hear the report echoing in the distance.

PART 3

THE PALISADES
January 12, 1943

13

How does one measure fidelity? In the war-torn Europe I've left behind fidelity has summoned death through its commitments. Lorca's world of Gypsies and peasants, lovers and visionaries, inflamed the mind of the Falange, poured acid into Valdés's ailing stomach until only Lorca's execution could staunch his pain. Fidelity to Saint Frederick, to his old father, drew Lorca back to Granada only to present him with the face of the man looking through the garden gate at the Huerta de San Vincente. But this apparent poverty is only an illusion, the truncated vision that comes to men looking through garden gates. Lorca's fidelity lay beyond the capacity of their eyes to a Spain they never dreamed of. Joaquín taught me that, and many other things besides.

207

I have had ample time to ponder the cost of fidelity since the flash from the rifle's muzzle and Joaquín's falling as the echo of the shot caromed through the mountains, trying to find its way back to penetrate his heart again in a superfluous coup de grâce. A month has passed since I wrote those words and heard the captain say that very night that we would reach San Francisco in the morning. I had entered his cabin steeped in particular grief fresh as a new wound, already wondering what reserves I could draw upon to finish this, tell how we carried Joaquín down the path and back to the station where, at dawn, a French police- man speaking in a low sympathetic voice explained that the Spaniards had quixotically lifted their restrictions and we were free to enter the country. It was he who confirmed what I word- lessly intuited even as Joaquín stumbled—that the shot was fired by a member of the Guardia Civil. Everything glittered with absurdity beneath the station lights. All I could think of was that if Lafont had not grown a smooth fur pelt, if Munch had not been murdered, we would have left Paris at the end of the week and found the border open, the gates swung accommodatingly wide, perhaps by the same man who fired the shot.

I wanted to say it all before the ship nosed its way along the docks and the same sailors who cast off the lines in Lisbon har- bor threw them to American stevedores, before the captain and his mates appeared on the bridge and looked on with satisfaction and relief, anticipating whatever pleasures waited them on shore. It was important to finish before those things happened because, from the moment I inscribed the first word of my life with Joaquín in this diary, I had anticipated that moment of closure, assumed that it would bring me some relief, that my final word would signal that I had prepared myself for a new life in a place I had yet to see.

That was why I rose at the first indication of light brighten- ing the porthole I had watched for hours. I dressed hastily and reached the deck just as the sky went from purple to red. It was too late. The sun touched the Farallon Islands, the spires of the

Golden Gate, the uppermost pastel houses on distant hills, offering a beautiful, bitter sight that sapped my will to write. Claude
and Monika came up not long afterward, joining me at the
forward railing where we watched America approach and felt
the chill of the great bridge's shadow as we glided silently beneath.

A month has passed since then during which I have had
neither the energy nor inclination to return to these pages. We
set out for Los Angeles a few days later in a car Claude bought
in San Francisco, explored the coves of Monterey, endured the
heat of midland valleys, spent the night in Santa Barbara. Toward noon the next day we crested a hill and the great flatness of
Los Angeles spread out before us, a city that went on and on,
stopping only at the base of the San Fernando Mountains. An
hour later we had reached our new home in a district called
Pacific Palisades, a stucco house in the Spanish style on the edge
of a cliff overlooking Santa Monica Bay. Claude had rented it
from a colleague who would be on sabbatical.

I have a room with a view of the sea, a garden, a redwood
deck where the breeze is refreshing. I have come out here every
day since we arrived, but this is the first time I have brought my
diary, not because I did not wish to finish, but because I did not
know what to say. Even as we sailed beneath the span of the
Golden Gate I realized that what I would have said if we had
had one more day at sea was false, that the mere facts of the
time after Joaquín's death were only facts. I had suffered a radical failure of understanding, misconstruing the nature of those
events as well as those in Lorca's poem, which I appropriated to
give my writing form. I knew immediately what I lacked was
knowledge of a broader context, the only one that matters as I
see it now. As had been the case with so much of Joaquín's story,
as well as my own, the direction came of its own accord, spon-
sored by the question of fidelity.

Several days went by before I discovered why I was drawn to
this deck and stayed here all day long. Now it seems simple

enough. I have exchanged my place on the ship for this one on
the cliff because it affords some continuity. I feel close to Lorca's
Gypsy here, but I needed what happened earlier this morning to
find the will to write. As I walked along the beach, thinking of
her plunging like a cormorant into the pool, I unlocked the
secret she withheld so long. Since the first day out from Lisbon I
have tried to see what she saw as she entered the water without a
splash. I imagined setting my foot upon the railing of that old
ship and stepping into thin air, her green my blue, her mountains my horizon, my diary the sister of Lorca's poem. This
morning, as I watched the waves roll in, I saw her secret in the
translucent curve of water colored like old glass. As it rose,
thinned, crested and began its fall toward shore, she reached up
and eased her lover from his bed, pulling him down into that
green world beyond the Guardia's reach to a place where the
dark roses of the wounds patterning his white shirt floated off
harmlessly. Those roses were her gift to me. Now I want to
return the gift, return it to Lorca and to Joaquín, for I know
where closure lies. Until I saw that wave I felt a hollowness
inside, as though my womb were filled with air flooding downward like a gust of wind, my body dry and sere as windblown
deserts are. But I was wrong. I was hollow, but not alone. I had
my voices and my places. Lorca. Joaquín. The Gypsy.

And so I return now to my place on the ship, conjure Spain
from frigid air as I steady myself against the ship's rise and fall.
The sound of the wind holds Fuente Grande as surely as clay
molds do bronze castings. I reach. Touch. Lorenzo's voice enters
my fingertips. Beyond the rose-colored façades of the Alhambra,
beyond the flower gardens and tile roofs of Granada, the plains
leading to Víznar and the barranca come into view. I hear Joaquín saying how he reached those terraces along the path bor-
dering Ainadamar, I hear the wind freshen and blow hard, sending leaves eddying along the path. It is the same wind that swept
inland from the Gulf of Almería to Fuente Grande the morning
of our departure from the Gare d'Austerlitz. All that day heavy

clouds obscure the Sierra de Harana, and the people of Víznar close their shutters, drawing in upon themselves like turtles retreating into shells. At La Colonia Lorca listens to rain drumming on the roof, hears the wind in the olive trees and pines. Lorenzo motions to the guitarists, and as he sings a shock of hair black as a raven's wing falls across his forehead. Firelight bronzes faces and clapping hands, lights up the expectation in all their eyes as the song ends with a thrumming rasgado. In the silence they see Joaquín enter the Gare d'Austerlitz, watch the train snake through white fields, through mist blanketing the farms and villages of Languedoc. They see the sky clear above Carcassonne until the ancient city glows pink as the Alhambra. As we reach Port Bou the storm blows away towards Seville, leaving a sky full of stars and a gypsy moon lighting Archbishop's Road. They consider his progress as he sets out across the fields blue as bruised moonlight and goes along the path leading into the mountains where the man on horseback, whose patent-leather hat glows like black ice, fires and pain flares in a single red rose across Joaquín's chest.

There is nothing but the impossibly bright moon in a sky swept clean by the storm. Claude leans over him, looking down from a great height. Then Monika. Me. He forces himself to see us, to see the pines, stately as the towers of Carcassonne, suddenly uprooted by the will of the moon. The moon embraces the towers, and as it sails away he sails too, looking down on Fuente Grande, where the moon shines in the pool of Ainadamar not as a beaten silver disk but as a thin pale woman dressed in white. He sees himself reflected in her eyes as she embraces the pool and olive groves, her arms floating as they circle Lorca and those who accompanied him on the paseo—Disocoro Gonzales, the schoolmaster, the banderillos, Cabezas and Mergal, Lorenzo. She weaves acequia, path, terraces and schoolhouse together in a design as intricate as that of a lace mantilla. For a moment Claude, Monika and I are there too, our voices soft, distant, urgent. Then our words fade until he is alone and he cannot hear my stifled cry as he makes his way along the path, drawn by music so faint that he recognizes neither the melody nor the instruments that make it. As he passes the olive groves where Valdés's face shines like a saffron sun, the rhythm of a cante hondo rises from the terraces. Lorenzo's voice catches on the grace notes and breaks free until it seems his words might float all the way to the rime-frost stars. He sees Lorca and the others gathered in the open space below the terrace, hears the music become livelier as the sound of horns fills the air with the brassy strains of a sardana.

Along Archbishop's Road, people dream of music and the sound of voices on the wind. Men in cantinas pause in their talk, setting aside their cards because they hear more than the faint trickling of water in the acequia running beside the road. Afterward the villagers of Víznar, as well as peasants in nearby farms, assert that a fire burned all that night in Fuente Grande.

About the Author

LAWRENCE THORNTON was born and educated in California where he lives with his wife. *Imagining Argentina,* his first novel, was chosen as one of the Notable Books of 1987 by *The New York Times* and received a number of literary prizes, including the Ernest Hemingway Foundation Award, the PEN American Center West Award for Best Novel of 1987, a nomination for the PEN/Faulkner Award, the Shirley Collier Award from UCLA and the Silver Medal of the Commonwealth Club of California. He recently received fellowships from the John Simon Guggenheim Foundation and the National Endowment for the Arts. His third novel, *Marlow's Book,* will appear next year. He is at work on a fourth.